Echoes Of Redemption Judas Unleashes Hell

Echoes Of Redemption Judas Unleashes Hell

DOug Hensley

Reece Hensley

Ingram spark

CONTENTS

Echoes Of Redemption
Judas Unleashes Hell
By
Doug Hensley

Table Of Contents

Chapter 8: Shadows in the Rooms The rooms of the mansion transform into forgotten tombs, where only the dead seem to walk in the shadows, driven by an otherworldly force.

Chapter 9: The Principal's Obsession The possessed principal becomes obsessed with gathering the coins, unknowingly playing into Judas' sinister plan.

Chapter 10: A Priest's Intuition Local Catholic priests sense the rising darkness and recognize the demonic threat, prompting them to seek assistance from the Vatican.

Chapter 11: The Call to Rome Disturbed by the unfolding events, the local priests reach out to Rome, seeking the expertise of the Vatican's best exorcists and demonologists.

Chapter 12: The Race Against Time The Vatican dispatches a team to stop the principal from collecting all 30 pieces of silver before Judas can return.

Chapter 13: Unveiling the Secrets A select few, including the priests and Vatican agents, unravel the hidden history of the coins and their potential to unleash Hell.

Chapter 14: Dark Forces at Play As the demonic powers intensify, the mansion becomes a battleground between the forces of good and the malevolent spirit of Judas.

Chapter 15: Protecting Mankind The Vatican team strategizes to thwart Judas' plan and prevent the principal from completing the unholy collection.

Chapter 16: Confrontation in the Shadows A climactic showdown ensues as the principal, now fully possessed, confronts the Vatican agents in a dark and foreboding corner of the mansion.

Chapter 17: Unleashing Hell Judas's influence reaches its peak, threatening to unleash Hell on Earth as the demonic power of the coins intensifies.

Chapter 18: The Power of Faith Amidst the chaos, the priests and Vatican agents rely on their faith and knowledge to combat the malevolence that seeks to engulf the world.

Chapter 19: Redemption or Damnation The fate of mankind hangs in the balance as the battle between good and evil reaches its zenith—will Judas be stopped, or will Hell be unleashed?

Chapter 20: The Aftermath In the aftermath, the mansion stands silent, and the principal's family grapples with the haunting memories of the supernatural ordeal that unfolded within its walls.

Author's Notes

In the gripping supernatural thriller, "Echoes of Redemption," a once-forgotten mansion becomes the epicenter of an otherworldly battle between light and shadow. When a new High School Principal and his family move into the abandoned home, they unknowingly unleash ancient curses and demonic forces tied to the disappearance of an archaeologist who had unearthed the thirty pieces of silver paid to Judas Iscariot. Possessed by the spirit of Judas, the Principal becomes a pawn in a cosmic game that could unleash Hell upon the world.

Local Catholic Priests, recognizing the imminent threat, call for assistance from Rome. Armed with artifacts holding ancient powers, the family, along with Samuel, must navigate the labyrinthine corridors of the haunted mansion, confronting malevolent entities, deciphering cryptic symbols, and making choices that echo through time.

As they unravel the secrets hidden within the mansion's depths, the family and Samuel discover the artifacts' ability to influence the forces of redemption or damnation. The echoes of the abyss resonate through the town's history, culminating in a climactic showdown during the Nexus Convergence—a celestial event that holds the key to the town's destiny.

Will the family and Samuel triumph over the shadows that haunt the mansion, or will Judas Iscariot succeed in unleashing Hell upon the world? "Echoes of Redemption" explores the timeless themes of choice, destiny, and the enduring power of redemption in a tale that seamlessly weaves supernatural suspense, ancient prophecies, and a quest for salvation. Brace yourself for a journey into the unknown, where the echoes of the abyss linger, and redemption awaits those who dare to confront the shadows.

Chapter 1: The Abandoned Mansion - Unveiling the Enigma

The abandoned mansion stood like a sentinel against the darkening sky, its once-grand facade now cloaked in an eerie silence. The wind whispered through the overgrown trees that surrounded the property, their gnarled branches casting ominous shadows on the cracked windows.

In the small town nearby, the tale of the vanished archaeologist echoed through hushed conversations. Dr. Jonathan Hargrove, a man of academic renown, had returned from a dig site in Israel, only to disappear without a trace. The townsfolk whispered of curses and ancient relics, but no one dared approach the mansion that had become synonymous with the professor's mysterious disappearance.

As the sun dipped below the horizon, the mansion seemed to absorb the encroaching darkness, its windows reflecting only shadows and secrets. Locals avoided the property like the plague, shrouded in superstitions that even the bravest dared not challenge.

Yet, curiosity has a way of luring even the most rational minds into the realm of the unknown. One evening, a group of adventurous teenagers decided to test their mettle and explore the forsaken mansion. Armed with flashlights and nervous laughter, they approached the imposing wrought-iron gates.

The creaking sound as the gates swung open echoed like a distant scream, but the thrill of the forbidden drew them further into the heart of the property. The mansion loomed ahead, its windows glistening with an otherworldly glow.

Inside, the air hung heavy with the scent of decay and dampness. The teenagers ventured cautiously through the dilapidated halls, their footsteps echoing in the emptiness. Dust-covered furniture loomed like spectral remnants of a bygone era, frozen in time.

As they entered the grand foyer, a sudden gust extinguished their flashlights, plunging them into pitch darkness. Panic set in as the oppressive silence was shattered by an otherworldly moan that seemed to emanate from the very walls of the mansion. Shadows danced in the corners of their vision, and cold fingers of dread traced their spines.

A distant whisper echoed through the darkness, "Leave this place," it murmured, a warning that resonated with the bone-chilling chill that now permeated the air.

The teenagers fumbled to relight their flashlights, but the darkness resisted their feeble attempts. Suddenly, the grand staircase, shrouded in darkness until now, became illuminated by an unseen force. The flickering light revealed a figure descending the stairs—a silhouette that seemed to materialize from the shadows themselves.

Frozen in terror, the intruders could only watch as the figure drew closer. The dim light revealed a spectral form, the face of Dr. Jonathan Hargrove twisted in anguish. His eyes bore into theirs, and a voice, not quite his own, spoke with a haunting resonance.

"You shouldn't have come," it intoned, the words echoing in the hollow chambers of the mansion. "This place is cursed, and the secrets it holds are not meant for the living."

The teenagers, paralyzed by fear, felt an unseen force pushing them towards the exit. As they stumbled out of the mansion, the gates swung shut with a deafening clang, sealing the cursed abode once more.

Back in the town, the group recounted their harrowing experience with trembling voices. The townsfolk listened in silence, their eyes widening with a mix of dread and disbelief. The legend of the abandoned mansion had taken on a new, terrifying dimension, and the name of Dr. Jonathan Hargrove became synonymous with the supernatural.

Little did they know, the mansion's dark secrets were destined to resurface, not in the whispers of frightened townsfolk, but in the unsuspecting lives of those who would soon call it home.

Chapter 2: A New Beginning - Embracing Shadows

The town slept under the shroud of night as a pale moon hung in the sky, casting an ethereal glow upon the silent streets. Unbeknownst to the residents, the ominous fate that clung to the abandoned mansion now awaited a new arrival.

John Harris, a seasoned educator known for his unassuming demeanor, had recently accepted the position of high school principal in the quiet town. Little did he realize that his compensation package included more than just a paycheck—it came with the keys to the forsaken mansion, a dwelling that seemed to have absorbed the sorrows of centuries.

As John, his wife Emma, and their two children, Lily and Ethan, approached the mansion, an unsettling feeling settled over them. The air felt thick with unseen eyes, and the once welcoming glow of the streetlights now seemed to flicker ominously.

The front door groaned as it swung open, revealing a cavernous foyer that echoed with the eerie whispers of the past. The family hesitated, exchanging uneasy glances, but the promise of a spacious home and the allure of a prestigious position propelled them forward.

The mansion's interior, now dimly lit by the family's tentative footsteps, seemed to pulse with a hidden energy. Dust particles danced in the air, catching stray beams of moonlight that filtered through the cracked windows. The walls, adorned with faded wallpaper, bore witness to the secrets etched into the very fabric of the mansion.

As they explored the rooms, the family's laughter echoed hollowly, bouncing off the walls like a desperate plea to break the silence that clung to the mansion. Lily, the younger of the Harris children, couldn't shake the feeling that unseen eyes followed her every move. She whispered her discomfort to Ethan, who dismissed it as childish imagination, but the unease lingered.

In the master bedroom, John and Emma felt a sudden drop in temperature, and a chill crawled up their spines. The atmosphere seemed charged with an otherworldly energy that intensified as they moved deeper into the mansion's secrets. Shadows seemed to dance on the walls, their movements disconnected from any discernible source.

As night fell, the family gathered in the dimly lit dining room, their voices hushed by the oppressive atmosphere. An unsettling quiet settled over the mansion, broken only by the distant howl of a lone wolf. Unbeknownst to them, the very fabric of the mansion pulsated with an ancient malevolence, eager to entangle their lives in the web of its sinister history.

As the clock struck midnight, a soft whisper echoed through the halls, barely audible but undeniably present. John, Emma, Lily, and Ethan exchanged wary glances, the weight of an invisible presence settling on their shoulders.

The mansion, like a dormant beast, waited patiently for its new occupants to succumb to the shadows that clung to its walls. Little did the Harris family know, their dreams of a new beginning would soon unravel in the face of a malevolent force that had long awaited its chance to awaken and manifest its unholy desires.

The night pressed on, and the mansion seemed to breathe, absorbing the fear and uncertainty that now clung to the Harris family. Unseen eyes watched from the shadows as the darkness embraced its newfound victims, setting the stage for a malevolent force to emerge from the depths of the abandoned mansion's haunted history.

Chapter 3: The Unaware Family - Shadows in the Halls

Days turned into nights within the mansion's oppressive embrace, and the Harris family, oblivious to the looming darkness, went about their lives with a false sense of normalcy. The once-cheerful atmosphere that accompanied moving into a new home now twisted into an unsettling quiet, a silence that echoed with hidden whispers and unseen footsteps.

In the heart of the mansion, shadows clung to the walls like malevolent specters, their movements synchronized with the pulse of an ancient force. Lily, the youngest of the Harris children, found solace in the small attic room she had claimed as her own. Little did she know that the attic, with its dusty trinkets and forgotten relics, held the key to the impending terror that would unfold.

Late one night, as the moon cast long, eerie shadows across the hallway, Lily heard a soft creaking sound. At first, she dismissed it as the settling of an old house, but a peculiar feeling gnawed at her senses. Hesitant but curious, she tiptoed into the dimly lit hallway, the air heavy with an unspoken dread.

As Lily approached her parents' bedroom, a chilling draft enveloped her. The door, ajar, seemed to beckon her closer. The family photos on the walls distorted into grimacing faces, and the once-welcoming bedroom felt like the threshold to an unknown realm. Lily, compelled by an unseen force, pushed the door open.

Inside, the room pulsed with an otherworldly energy. Shadows writhed on the walls, forming grotesque shapes that seemed to reach out for her. The air grew colder, and Lily's breath hung in front of her like a spectral fog. In the center of the room, her parents lay still, trapped in an unnatural slumber.

Lily, paralyzed by fear, felt the temperature drop further. Whispers echoed through the room, unintelligible but filled with a malevolent intent. The shadows seemed to gather around her, closing in like predatory beasts. In a desperate attempt to break free, she stumbled backward, her voice caught in her throat.

Downstairs, John and Emma slept soundly, oblivious to the supernatural forces at play. The mansion, now fully awakened, hungered for their unwitting participation in the impending nightmare. Lily, haunted by the spectral encounter, dared not speak of the unnatural cold that clung to her.

As days turned into nights, the family's routine became a delicate dance with the unknown. Ethan, the older sibling, began to notice subtle changes in Lily's behavior. She spoke in hushed tones, her eyes haunted by a terror she couldn't articulate. When he pressed her for an explanation, she dismissed it as overactive imagination, yet the unease persisted.

In the depths of the mansion, the shadows whispered their secrets, and the ancient force that lay dormant reveled in the family's unwitting descent into its clutches. The once-grand halls transformed into a labyrinth of hidden corridors and forbidden chambers, each step leading the Harris family closer to the precipice of an unimaginable abyss.

The mansion, now a living entity, toyed with their perceptions. Shadows seemed to move independently, objects shifted without cause, and the very walls pulsated with a malevolent heartbeat. A sense of foreboding lingered in the air, a warning that went unnoticed by the unsuspecting family.

As the darkness deepened, the mansion's grip tightened, weaving its tendrils around their lives. Unseen eyes watched their every move, and the whispers in the halls grew louder, a symphony of spectral voices converging on the unwitting occupants of the once-abandoned mansion. The stage was set for a nightmarish revelation that would shatter the illusion of normalcy, plunging the Harris family into a terrifying reality they could never have anticipated.

Chapter 4: Whispers in the Halls - Echoes of the Damned

Nightfall draped the mansion in an inky blackness, and the air inside seemed charged with an otherworldly presence. As the Harris family settled into an uneasy sleep, the mansion awoke, its long-forgotten secrets stirring in the shadows.

In the dead of night, Emma Harris awoke to a disconcerting sound—a soft, haunting melody that seemed to seep through the walls. The tune, if it could be called that, danced on the edge of perception, a ghostly hum that wormed its way into her dreams. As she lay there, the once-familiar contours of the bedroom twisted into grotesque shapes, and the moonlight painted sinister patterns on the walls.

Unsure whether the melody originated from some external source or was a figment of her imagination, Emma roused her husband, John. His eyes flickered open, and the disquiet that clouded Emma's gaze mirrored his own unease. The melody persisted, a spectral symphony that echoed through the corridors like a harbinger of unseen terrors.

Together, they ventured into the hallway, their steps muffled by an unnatural silence. The mansion seemed to breathe, its ancient pulse quickening in tandem with their hesitant movements. The melody led them through winding corridors and forgotten alcoves, its source elusive like a phantom in the night.

As they approached the grand staircase, the melody reached a crescendo, filling the air with a haunting beauty that belied its malevolent origins. Shadows danced on the walls, their movements synchronized with the spectral notes that seemed to emanate from the very heart of the mansion.

Descending the staircase, the couple entered the grand foyer, where the melody reached its zenith. In the center of the room, a dim glow materialized—a ghostly figure, draped in shadows, playing an ethereal tune on a long-forgotten piano. The figure, translucent yet vivid, turned towards them, its eyes empty voids that seemed to pierce their very souls.

Emma gasped, her breath catching in her throat. The ghostly pianist, a manifestation of the mansion's malevolence, continued its haunting melody, the notes resonating with an otherworldly power that tugged at the fabric of reality itself.

Unable to tear their gaze away, John and Emma felt the weight of an unseen force pressing down on them. The walls seemed to close in, and the air became dense with an oppressive energy. The once-elegant furniture, now twisted into contorted shapes, bore witness to the spectral performance that held the couple captive.

In the midst of the haunting melody, the mansion's pulse quickened, and the ghostly pianist's eyes flashed with an unholy fervor. The couple, ensnared by the supernatural spectacle, felt tendrils of malevolence slither into their minds, weaving dark thoughts and unsettling visions.

As the last haunting note lingered in the air, the ghostly figure dissolved into shadows, leaving the couple standing in the grand foyer, shaken to their core. The melody lingered in their minds like an indelible stain, a constant reminder of the malevolent force that had woven its influence into the very fabric of the mansion.

The following days blurred into a disorienting haze. John and Emma, haunted by the spectral encounter, struggled to maintain a facade of normalcy for the sake of their children. Unbeknownst to them, the mansion reveled in their vulnerability, its ancient tendrils tightening their grip on the unwitting occupants.

Lily, the youngest of the Harris children, began to exhibit strange behavior. She spoke of unseen figures in the corners of her room, shadows that whispered forbidden secrets. The once-lively girl now seemed like a vessel for the supernatural, her eyes reflecting a terror that transcended the ordinary fears of childhood.

Ethan, the older sibling, dismissed his sister's claims as overactive imagination. However, he too felt the oppressive atmosphere that clung to the mansion. The walls seemed to murmur secrets, and the air hummed with an unnatural energy that set his nerves on edge.

In the dead of night, as the family slept in restless slumber, the mansion came alive with whispered conversations that echoed through the halls. Shadows, animated by an unseen force, gathered in the corners like conspirators plotting a malevolent scheme. The very fabric of the mansion seemed to ripple with an ancient knowledge, a sinister truth that remained just beyond the family's grasp.

Unbeknownst to the Harris family, the melody that had ensnared Emma and John was a prelude to the malevolent forces that lurked within the mansion's depths. The spectral pianist, a harbinger of unseen terrors, had merely opened the gateway to a nightmarish symphony that would soon envelop their lives in a cacophony of horror and despair.

As the days turned into a nightmarish procession, the mansion's shadows whispered of a darkness that sought to consume them. Unseen eyes watched their every move, and the air crackled with an impending malevolence. The Harris family, oblivious to the abyss that yawned beneath the surface of their newfound home, teetered on the brink of a descent into the depths of supernatural horror. The mansion, a malevolent puppeteer, reveled in their unwitting participation in a ghastly dance that would soon spiral into a nightmare from which there might be no awakening.

Chapter 5: Possession Unleashed - Dance of the Damned

As the sun dipped below the horizon, casting long shadows across the mansion's desolate grounds, an ancient malevolence stirred within its walls. The spectral melody that had haunted the Harris family lingered in the air like a discordant echo, foreshadowing the horrors yet to unfold.

That night, the Harris family slept fitfully, ensnared in a realm where dreams intertwined with the supernatural. In the depths of their restless slumber, a shadowy figure emerged from the darkness, slipping through the corridors like a phantom on a malevolent mission.

John Harris, the unsuspecting high school principal, became the target of the malevolence that lurked within the mansion. As he dreamed, his subconscious mind became a battleground for unseen forces, a realm where reality and nightmare melded into a surreal tapestry.

In his dreams, John found himself standing in a dimly lit chamber, surrounded by ancient symbols etched into the walls. The air crackled with an unnatural energy, and the distant echoes of whispers reverberated through the chamber like the distant cries of tormented souls.

Before him stood a spectral figure, its features shrouded in darkness. The figure extended a hand, revealing a twisted smile that seemed to carve itself into John's very soul. The air thickened with an oppressive force as the figure spoke in a voice that echoed with an otherworldly resonance.

"John Harris," it intoned, the words carrying an ominous weight. "You have entered a realm where shadows dance with the damned. Embrace the darkness that beckons, for you are the vessel through which ancient malevolence shall be unleashed."

The dream shifted, and John found himself standing in the grand foyer of the mansion. Shadows gathered around him, coalescing into a nightmarish dance that seemed to mock the laws of reality. The whispers that had once lingered in the background now crescendoed into a cacophony of unholy voices.

A sense of dread gripped John as he moved through the mansion in his dream, guided by an unseen force. The walls seemed to pulse with a malevolent heartbeat, and the air became suffused with the stench of decay. The once-familiar rooms twisted into grotesque shapes, their contents warped by an unseen hand.

In the attic, Lily, the young daughter, slept fitfully, her dreams haunted by visions of ancient coins and the ghostly pianist. In the corridors, Emma and Ethan experienced a shared nightmare, where the mansion's walls seemed to close in, trapping them in an endless labyrinth of shadows.

The dreamworld and the waking world began to blur, and John, trapped within the nightmarish dance, felt the boundaries of reality dissolve. The mansion, a malevolent puppeteer, wove its tendrils into the very fabric of his consciousness, tainting his thoughts with an insidious influence.

As dawn approached, John awoke in a cold sweat, the residual echoes of the dream lingering like a sinister aftertaste. Unbeknownst to him, the malevolence that had seized his subconscious now sought to manifest itself in the waking world.

In the days that followed, a subtle change overcame John. His once steady gaze now bore a flicker of distant emptiness, and a disquieting calm settled over him. Unseen eyes watched his every move, and the mansion's ancient force, having tasted the vulnerability within his dreams, sought to solidify its hold on the unsuspecting principal.

The spectral figure from John's dream, a manifestation of an ancient malevolence, lingered in the shadows, observing with a twisted satisfaction. The atmosphere within the mansion crackled with an unholy tension, and the whispers in the halls grew more insistent, a chorus of voices urging the inevitable descent into darkness.

As John navigated the corridors of the mansion, his footsteps seemed synchronized with an unseen rhythm—an ancient dance that echoed the sinister forces at play. Unbeknownst to his family, he became a vessel for an entity that hungered for release, a force that sought to break the shackles of its long-forgotten prison.

One evening, as the sun dipped below the horizon, casting long shadows that stretched like skeletal fingers across the mansion's grounds, the malevolence within John awakened. The family, oblivious to the impending horror, gathered for a seemingly ordinary dinner in the dimly lit dining room.

As the night wore on, the mansion's pulse quickened, and the atmosphere became charged with an unholy energy. John, his eyes vacant, rose from the dinner table, guided by an unseen force. His family, their expressions a mix of concern and confusion, watched in silence as he moved with an unnatural grace.

In the grand foyer, John's body became a vessel for the malevolent force that sought to manifest itself in the waking world. The shadows gathered around him, their movements synchronized with an ancient dance that defied the laws of nature.

The spectral figure, now visible to the naked eye, emerged from the darkness. Its eyes, pools of emptiness, bore into John's soul. The air thickened with a sense of impending doom as the figure spoke in a voice that echoed through the corridors.

"John Harris, you are the key to the unleashing of ancient malevolence. Embrace your destiny, for the dance of the damned has begun."

The family, paralyzed by a mixture of fear and disbelief, could only watch as John, seemingly in a trance, moved towards a hidden chamber within the mansion. The air crackled with an unholy energy, and the very walls seemed to pulsate with an ancient heartbeat.

As John entered the chamber, the door swung shut behind him with a resounding thud. The family, gripped by an indescribable terror, rushed towards the sealed entrance, but an unseen force repelled their attempts to break through.

Inside the chamber, John found himself surrounded by ancient symbols and cryptic markings. The air hummed with a malevolent resonance, and the room seemed to exist outside the boundaries of time and space. Shadows danced on the walls, forming grotesque shapes that seemed to mock the very fabric of reality.

In the center of the chamber, a pedestal stood, upon which rested a single ancient coin—the first of the thirty pieces of silver that had once belonged to Judas Iscariot. As John approached the coin, the malevolent force within the mansion intensified, wrapping itself around him like a suffocating shroud.

Unbeknownst to the family, the chamber held the key to an ancient prophecy—the awakening of Judas Iscariot, a malevolent force that had long slumbered in the depths of Hell. The coins, each possessing a demonic power, were scattered throughout the mansion, waiting to be gathered by the unwitting principal.

As John touched the first coin, a surge of dark energy coursed through him. His eyes, once vacant, now burned with an unholy fervor. The chamber became a nexus of malevolence, a focal point for the forces that sought to break free from the shackles of centuries.

Outside the sealed chamber, the family, their desperation mounting, could only listen to the muffled echoes of an otherworldly chant that emanated from within. The mansion seemed to groan in response, its very foundation shaken by the malevolent dance unfolding in its hidden recesses.

As the night wore on, the family, their minds clouded by a sense of impending doom, struggled to find a way to break through the sealed entrance. Emma, her eyes filled with terror, frantically searched for any sign of help within the dimly lit foyer. Ethan, fueled by a mixture of fear and determination, tried in vain to force the chamber door open.

Meanwhile, Lily, the youngest of the Harris family, stood in the shadows, her gaze fixed on the sealed entrance. Unbeknownst to her family, she had become attuned to the supernatural currents that pulsed through the mansion. Whispers echoed in her ears, urging her to uncover the truth that lurked in the shadows.

In the chamber, John Harris, now a vessel for the malevolent force, continued the ominous chant that reverberated through the walls. The ancient coin in his hand seemed to throb with an otherworldly power, its malevolence resonating with the dark forces that sought to break free.

As the chant reached its zenith, the mansion's foundations shook, and the air crackled with an intensity that transcended the natural realm. Shadows coalesced around John, forming a grotesque silhouette that seemed to merge with the very essence of the chamber.

Outside, the family gasped as the sealed entrance began to crack, as if the very walls of the mansion rebelled against the ancient malevolence. The spectral figure, the harbinger of the dark forces at play, appeared in the grand foyer. Its eyes, now ablaze with an unholy light, surveyed the scene with a malevolent satisfaction.

"The dance has begun," it whispered, the words carrying through the air like a curse. "The coins awaken, and the gateway to darkness opens."

The family, their faces etched with fear, watched as the entrance to the chamber swung open, revealing a tableau of supernatural horror. John, his eyes now pools of emptiness, stood at the center of the chamber, surrounded by swirling shadows that seemed to defy the laws of nature.

Ethan, Emma, and Lily, drawn by an otherworldly force, entered the chamber, their footsteps echoing in the surreal silence. The atmosphere within the room crackled with an ancient malevolence, and the coins, scattered across the chamber like forbidden artifacts, pulsed with an unholy energy.

As the family approached, John extended his hand, offering them the first of the thirty coins. The malevolent force within the mansion whispered in their minds, urging them to embrace the dark power that awaited them. Emma hesitated, her instincts warring with the unnatural influence that clouded her thoughts.

Lily, however, seemed entranced by the coins, her eyes reflecting a mixture of curiosity and an innate connection to the supernatural.

Unbeknownst to the others, she had become a conduit for the ancient forces that sought to manipulate the fate of the Harris family.

Ethan, torn between his love for his family and the insidious pull of the malevolent force, reached for the coin with trembling hands. As the cool metal touched his skin, a surge of dark energy coursed through him, intertwining with the very fabric of his being.

The room seemed to warp and twist, its dimensions shifting as the ancient forces gained strength. Shadows danced on the walls, forming grotesque shapes that seemed to writhe with an unseen malevolence. The spectral figure, now fully manifested, observed the unfolding ritual with a triumphant gaze.

In the midst of the supernatural maelstrom, the family, now tethered to the dark forces that pulsed through the mansion, began a macabre dance—a dance of possession, where the boundaries between the living and the damned blurred into a nightmarish tableau.

As the ritual reached its climax, the mansion itself seemed to sigh with an unholy satisfaction. The air crackled with malevolent energy, and the shadows that clung to the walls whispered in a chorus of demonic voices. The family, now entangled in the ancient prophecy, had unwittingly become pawns in a supernatural game that transcended the boundaries of time and space.

The night wore on, and the mansion, now a conduit for the forces of darkness, embraced its newfound role in the unfolding nightmare. The malevolence that had lain dormant for centuries now surged through the halls, its influence reaching beyond the confines of the once-abandoned mansion.

The townsfolk, oblivious to the supernatural drama that unfolded within the mansion, felt an unexplained unease settle over the town. The air hung heavy with an ominous presence, and whispers of an ancient evil spread through the streets like a contagion.

As the first light of dawn approached, the mansion, now a bastion of supernatural malevolence, stood silent, its halls echoing with the lingering remnants of the unholy ritual. The family, forever changed by the dance of possession, remained within the grasp of the dark forces that now held sway over their lives.

The mansion, having served its purpose as a vessel for the awakening of ancient malevolence, waited patiently for the next chapter of the nightmare to unfold. The town, unaware of the impending doom that loomed on the horizon, remained shrouded in an eerie stillness—a stillness that hinted at the malevolent forces that now pulsed within the heart of the once-abandoned mansion.

Chapter 6: A Dig Site Revelation - Unveiling the Shadows

The town lay beneath a pall of unease as the malevolent forces within the mansion continued to pulse with an ancient energy. Unbeknownst to the residents, the tendrils of darkness reached beyond the confines of the foreboding estate, casting a sinister shadow that loomed over the unsuspecting town.

While the town slept in the clutches of an uneasy stillness, a figure emerged from the shadows—a local historian named Samuel Green, whose research into the town's history had unearthed whispers of an ancient curse. Samuel, drawn by an insatiable curiosity, sensed that the key to the town's torment lay within the abandoned mansion.

As he approached the looming structure, the air grew thick with an unseen malevolence. Samuel hesitated but pressed on, his footsteps echoing through the deserted streets. The mansion, now a beacon of supernatural power, seemed to welcome his arrival with a silent promise of revelation.

In the grand foyer, Samuel felt an oppressive force settle over him, as if the very air conspired to keep its secrets. The whispers that had haunted the town now seemed to converge within the mansion, echoing through the hallways like a chorus of tormented souls.

Driven by an unrelenting determination, Samuel ascended the grand staircase, guided by an unseen force that seemed to draw him towards an ancient truth. The mansion, now fully awakened, seemed to shift and contort as if it were a living entity, eager to reveal its long-buried secrets.

As he explored the upper floors, Samuel's senses heightened. He could feel the weight of unseen eyes upon him, and the air seemed charged with an ancient energy that sent shivers down his spine. The once-forgotten rooms, now transformed by the malevolent forces at play, whispered tales of a dark history that had long been obscured by the passage of time.

In an abandoned study, Samuel stumbled upon a dusty collection of old manuscripts and journals. As he perused the fragile pages, he uncovered the history of the mansion and the curse that had plagued the town for generations. The ink on the pages seemed to writhe with a life of its own, as if the very words sought to convey the gravity of the malevolence that lingered within.

The tale began centuries ago, with a mysterious cult that had sought forbidden knowledge and dark powers. Legends spoke of an artifact— an ancient relic that held the essence of a malevolent force. The cult, drawn by the promise of unimaginable power, had conducted a ritual within the very mansion that now stood as a monument to their malevolent pursuits.

As Samuel delved deeper into the history, he uncovered the identity of the cult's leader—a figure shrouded in darkness, a puppeteer who had manipulated the threads of supernatural forces. The name Judas Iscariot surfaced repeatedly, and with each revelation, the air within the study seemed to grow heavier.

The cult's ritual, described in painstaking detail within the fragile pages, involved the gathering of thirty pieces of silver. Each coin, imbued with a demonic power, held the key to awakening a malevolent force—a force that had long remained dormant but sought to return to the mortal realm.

As Samuel absorbed the chilling details, a sudden realization struck him—the curse that had tormented the town was not a mere superstition but a living manifestation of an ancient evil. The thirty pieces of silver, scattered throughout the mansion, were conduits for a malevolent force that sought to return from the depths of Hell.

Determined to unveil the truth, Samuel descended into the bowels of the mansion, guided by the whispers that now seemed to emanate from the very walls. The shadows gathered around him, forming grotesque shapes that seemed to echo the torment of the souls ensnared within the mansion's dark history.

In a hidden chamber, Samuel discovered an ancient altar adorned with cryptic symbols. The air hummed with an unnatural energy as he approached, drawn by an unseen force. On the altar, he found a single ancient coin—the same coin that John Harris, now possessed by the malevolent force, had touched to initiate the nightmarish dance.

As Samuel reached for the coin, the chamber seemed to come alive with a malevolent force. The walls pulsed with dark energy, and the shadows coalesced into a spectral figure—a manifestation of the ancient evil that had long awaited its return. The whispers in the chamber grew louder, echoing a language that transcended the mortal realm.

"Samuel Green," the spectral figure intoned, its voice a haunting echo. "You have unveiled the shadows that cloak this cursed mansion. Yet, the dance of possession has begun, and the forces that lie dormant seek to consume all within their grasp."

Samuel, undeterred by the supernatural spectacle, felt a surge of determination. The ancient evil, now fully aware of his presence, sought to manipulate his thoughts and fears. The whispers echoed tales of doom, of an impending darkness that would swallow the town whole.

As Samuel clutched the ancient coin, a surge of dark energy coursed through him. The chamber seemed to warp and twist, its dimensions bending to the will of the malevolent force. Shadows danced on the walls, forming grotesque shapes that seemed to mock the very fabric of reality.

Unbeknownst to Samuel, the spectral figure that stood before him bore witness to the unfolding events within the mansion. The dance of possession, initiated by the unwitting Harris family, now threatened to entangle Samuel in its nightmarish grasp.

The town, still shrouded in an eerie stillness, remained oblivious to the supernatural drama that played out within the mansion's walls. The malevolent force, having tasted the vulnerability of its new puppet, sought to manipulate Samuel's every move, drawing him deeper into the labyrinth of shadows.

As Samuel descended further into the mansion's depths, the ancient evil whispered tales of an impending apocalypse—a revelation that would unleash Hell upon the town and beyond. The shadows that clung to the walls seemed to writhe with anticipation, eager to witness the culmination of centuries-old machinations.

Back in the chamber, the spectral figure, its eyes ablaze with unholy fervor, watched as Samuel succumbed to the influence of the ancient coin. The very air seemed to vibrate with an otherworldly power, and the mansion itself groaned in response to the malevolent forces at play.

The dance of possession, initiated by the unwitting Harris family, now unfolded on a grander scale. Samuel, his mind a battleground for supernatural forces, moved with an unnatural grace as he navigated the twisting corridors of the mansion. Unseen eyes watched his every move, and the shadows whispered in a chorus of demonic voices.

In the grand foyer, Samuel encountered the spectral figure once more. Its form seemed to shift and contort, mirroring the malevolent forces that now pulsed through the mansion. The whispers in the air formed a sinister symphony, a cacophony of tormented souls that echoed the impending doom.

"You are but a pawn in the dance of possession," the figure intoned, its voice reverberating through the halls. "The forces that have awakened seek to transcend the boundaries of Hell and Earth. The town, the mansion, and all who dwell within shall bear witness to the unveiling of shadows."

Samuel, now fully entranced by the malevolent forces, continued his descent into the heart of the mansion. The ancient coin, clutched in his hand, seemed to guide his every step, leading him towards a revelation that would reshape the fabric of reality itself.

As the night wore on, the town remained cloaked in an ominous silence, unaware of the supernatural forces that now converged within the mansion. The malevolent energy, having seized control of Samuel, sought to manipulate the threads of fate, weaving a tapestry of horror that transcended the boundaries of mortal understanding.

The once-abandoned mansion, now a crucible of malevolence, awaited the culmination of its dark purpose. The shadows that clung to its walls seemed to pulse with an ancient heartbeat, resonating with the whispers that echoed through its haunted halls. The dance of possession, initiated by the unwitting touch of an ancient coin, now unfolded with a relentless intensity—a nightmare that would soon engulf the town in a maelstrom of supernatural horror.

Chapter 7: The Unraveling Night - Echoes of Damnation

As Samuel Green, now a puppet entwined in the malevolent dance, descended deeper into the mansion's shadows, the tendrils of darkness gripped his psyche with an unrelenting force. The ancient coin, clutched tightly in his hand, pulsed with an unholy energy that seemed to synchronize with the very heartbeat of the mansion.

In the dimly lit corridors, the air crackled with malevolent whispers that guided Samuel's every step. The shadows seemed to stretch and contort, forming grotesque shapes that danced with an eerie grace. The mansion, a living entity fueled by supernatural forces, groaned under the weight of an impending revelation.

The spectral figure, the harbinger of doom, trailed behind Samuel, its form shifting between shadows as it observed the puppet it had ensnared. The very air seemed to vibrate with an otherworldly resonance, and the whispers echoed with tales of an ancient prophecy—the awakening of Judas Iscariot and the impending descent of Hell upon the mortal realm.

Unbeknownst to Samuel, the townsfolk, still shrouded in an uneasy stillness, began to sense a palpable change in the atmosphere. A collective unease settled over the community, and rumors of a malevolent force emanating from the mansion circulated through hushed conversations.

The air itself seemed to carry an unnatural chill, a harbinger of the impending darkness that loomed on the horizon.

As Samuel reached the mansion's subterranean depths, he found himself standing before a foreboding door—etched with ancient symbols that seemed to writhe with an unholy life. The whispers in the air grew louder, urging him to open the portal that led to the heart of the malevolence that sought release.

With a trembling hand, Samuel pushed open the door, revealing a chamber that seemed to defy the laws of space and time. The air within vibrated with an otherworldly power, and the shadows danced with an eerie anticipation. At the center of the chamber, an altar stood, upon which rested the remaining twenty-nine pieces of silver.

The spectral figure materialized beside Samuel, its eyes ablaze with an unholy light. "The time has come," it intoned, its voice resonating with an ancient power. "Complete the ritual, and the ancient malevolence shall be unleashed upon the world."

Compelled by a force beyond his control, Samuel approached the altar. The ancient coins seemed to pulse with a malevolent energy, each one bearing the weight of an unholy history. The whispers in the chamber grew into a cacophony, a symphony of demonic voices that echoed the impending doom.

One by one, Samuel placed the remaining coins on the altar. With each coin added, the air crackled with dark energy, and the shadows in the chamber seemed to writhe in ecstasy. The malevolent force, now fully awakened, reached out to the coins, absorbing their demonic power.

As the ritual reached its climax, the mansion itself seemed to groan, its very foundation shaking with an otherworldly resonance. The town, still unaware of the supernatural horrors unfolding within the mansion, bore witness to an eclipse of the moon—an event foretold by ancient prophecies as a harbinger of impending darkness.

Back in the town, the unease that had settled over the community escalated into a palpable fear. The night took on a surreal quality, the shadows stretching and contorting with an unnatural life of their own. Whispers of an ancient curse echoed through the deserted streets, and the townsfolk, unable to shake the ominous feeling that hung in the air, locked themselves indoors.

Within the mansion's subterranean chamber, the ritual neared its conclusion. Samuel, now a vessel for the malevolent force, felt the ancient evil course through his veins. His eyes, once filled with curiosity, now burned with an unholy fervor as he completed the final steps of the dark ceremony.

The altar, now bathed in an eerie glow, seemed to resonate with the very heartbeat of the malevolent force. The chamber's walls pulsed with shadows that gathered around Samuel, forming a spectral vortex that seemed to tear through the fabric of reality itself.

In the grand foyer above, the Harris family, still entrapped in the supernatural dance, felt the mansion's foundations quake. Ethan, Emma, and Lily, their eyes vacant, moved with an unnatural grace as they descended towards the subterranean depths, drawn by an unseen force.

As the family reached the chamber, the spectral figure that had guided Samuel now stood at the forefront of the malevolent vortex. Its form contorted, merging with the shadows in a macabre dance. The air within the chamber vibrated with an intensity that transcended the mortal realm.

"The time of reckoning is at hand," the figure declared, its voice echoing through the chamber. "The dance of possession has woven the threads of fate, and the ancient malevolence shall be unleashed upon the world."

As the ritual reached its zenith, the very fabric of reality seemed to tear open. The town, still cloaked in an ominous silence, bore witness to a convergence of supernatural forces that eclipsed the boundaries of mortal understanding. The eclipse of the moon deepened, casting an eerie glow over the town's deserted streets.

In the subterranean chamber, the malevolent vortex expanded, its tendrils reaching beyond the confines of the mansion. The shadows, now imbued with an ancient power, spilled into the town like a malevolent tide. Unseen eyes watched from the darkness as the supernatural forces, unleashed by the unwitting actions of the Harris family and Samuel Green, sought to envelop the world in a nightmarish embrace.

The townsfolk, their fears realized, cowered within their homes as the malevolent shadows seeped through the cracks and crevices. Whispers echoed through the deserted streets, carrying tales of damnation and an impending apocalypse. The air itself seemed to vibrate with an unholy energy, and the very ground beneath the town quivered in response to the supernatural onslaught.

In the subterranean chamber, the spectral figure and the Harris family, now fully entwined in the malevolent dance, became conduits for the ancient evil that sought release. The vortex of shadows pulsed with a malevolent power, drawing the town into its nightmarish embrace.

As the final echoes of the dark ritual reverberated through the mansion, a portal opened within the chamber—a gateway between the mortal realm and the depths of Hell. The air crackled with infernal energy, and the very walls seemed to bleed with the essence of damnation.

From the depths of the portal, a figure emerged—an entity shrouded in darkness, its form indistinct yet radiating an aura of malevolence. The town, now fully ensnared in the supernatural maelstrom, quivered as the ancient evil materialized in the mortal realm.

The figure, a manifestation of Judas Iscariot, stood at the epicenter of the malevolent vortex. Its eyes, pools of emptiness, surveyed the town with a triumphant gaze. The eclipse of the moon reached its zenith, casting the town in an unholy glow that seemed to sear the very fabric of reality.

"The dance is complete," Judas Iscariot declared, his voice echoing through the town. "The shadows have embraced the mortal realm, and Hell itself shall walk among the living."

The townsfolk, now fully aware of the impending darkness, watched in horror as the entity known as Judas Iscariot extended his hand, summoning the malevolent shadows to coalesce around him. The very air seemed to scream in agony as the town became a battleground for the forces of damnation.

In the subterranean chamber, the spectral figure and the Harris family, their minds trapped in a nightmarish dance, served as vessels for the malevolent force. The portal, now fully open, emitted an otherworldly glow that bathed the chamber in an infernal light.

The entity of Judas Iscariot, having fully materialized, stepped through the portal and onto the streets of the town. The ground beneath his feet withered and blackened, and the air crackled with an intensity that heralded the arrival of an ancient evil.

The townsfolk, their faces etched with terror, fled from the malevolent shadows that now roamed the streets like vengeful spirits. The very essence of damnation had descended upon the town, and the supernatural forces, unleashed by the unwitting actions of the Harris family and Samuel Green, sought to rewrite the fabric of reality itself.

As Judas Iscariot surveyed the chaos that unfolded, a wicked smile played upon his lips. The ancient prophecy, woven through centuries of manipulation and dark rituals, had finally come to fruition. The town, now a battlefield between Hell and Earth, stood on the precipice of an unending night—a night where the echoes of damnation reverberated through the very soul of the once-innocent community.

Chapter 8: Veil of Desolation - Echoes in the Abyss

The once-quiet town now stood at the epicenter of a supernatural cataclysm. The malevolent forces unleashed by the ritual within the mansion had plunged the streets into an otherworldly chaos. Shadows, imbued with the essence of damnation, slithered through the deserted streets, reaching into every nook and cranny with an insatiable hunger.

Judas Iscariot, his form wreathed in darkness, strode through the town with an unholy purpose. The ground beneath his every step withered and decayed, leaving a trail of desolation in his wake. The malevolent shadows, now under his command, twisted and contorted like maleficent specters eager to fulfill their dark master's bidding.

The townsfolk, their faces etched with terror, scattered in all directions, seeking refuge from the encroaching darkness. The air vibrated with an unnatural resonance, and the once-familiar streets became a surreal labyrinth, where reality and nightmare intertwined.

Ethan, Emma, Lily, and Samuel, still ensnared in the malevolent dance, moved with an eerie grace through the chaos. Their vacant eyes bore witness to the horrors that unfolded, yet their actions remained dictated by the unseen forces that had bound them to the ancient ritual.

As the family and Samuel approached the heart of the town, the malevolent shadows seemed to coalesce into grotesque shapes that mirrored their deepest fears. Unseen whispers echoed in their minds, urging them to embrace the darkness and fulfill the prophecy that had long been foretold.

Judas Iscariot, the puppeteer of damnation, observed the family's descent into the abyss with a malevolent satisfaction. The town, now an extension of Hell itself, quivered under the weight of the supernatural forces that pulsed through its very foundations.

The townsfolk, their attempts to escape thwarted by the malevolent shadows, found themselves corralled towards the town square—an ancient cobblestone expanse that now served as the stage for an infernal spectacle. The spectral figure that had guided Samuel, now fully merged with the malevolent vortex, watched from the shadows, its form a silhouette against the backdrop of nightmarish chaos.

In the town square, the ground trembled as the malevolent forces gathered in anticipation of the next act in the unfolding nightmare. The entity of Judas Iscariot stood at the center, his eyes ablaze with an unholy light. The air crackled with infernal energy as he extended his hand, summoning the shadows to dance in a grotesque display.

Ethan, Emma, Lily, and Samuel, their movements dictated by an unseen force, stepped forward with an eerie synchronicity. The malevolent shadows intertwined with their forms, creating a spectral dance that seemed to defy the laws of nature. The townsfolk, ensnared in the nightmarish spectacle, could only watch in horror as the family and Samuel became vessels for the ancient evil that sought release.

As the dance unfolded, the air resonated with an otherworldly melody—a symphony of torment that echoed the very essence of damnation. The malevolent vortex pulsed with a dark energy, its tendrils reaching towards the heavens as if seeking to tear through the veil that separated Hell from Earth.

The townsfolk, their minds clouded by an otherworldly influence, felt a sense of despair settle over them. The very fabric of reality seemed to unravel, and the town square became a battleground where the forces of Hell clashed with the remnants of human consciousness.

In the midst of the infernal dance, a figure emerged from the shadows—an elderly priest, adorned in tattered vestments. Father Matthias, a beacon of faith in the face of damnation, stepped into the town square with a solemn determination. His eyes, hardened by a lifetime of spiritual battles, surveyed the unfolding chaos with an unwavering resolve.

"Evil has taken root within this town, but the light of faith shall prevail," Father Matthias declared, his voice cutting through the supernatural cacophony. "I stand as a guardian against the forces that seek to plunge us into darkness."

As the townsfolk, their attention momentarily diverted, witnessed the arrival of the priest, a glimmer of hope ignited within their hearts. Father Matthias, armed with a crucifix and an ancient tome, approached the malevolent vortex with a steely determination.

Judas Iscariot, his eyes narrowing with disdain, turned his attention towards the elderly priest. The malevolent shadows recoiled in the presence of the crucifix, revealing a momentary vulnerability within the supernatural maelstrom.

"You are a relic of a fading era, priest," Judas Iscariot sneered, his voice carrying the weight of centuries. "Your faith cannot withstand the impending darkness that I bring."

Undeterred, Father Matthias raised the crucifix, its radiant glow pushing back the encroaching shadows. He began chanting ancient incantations, calling upon the divine forces to lend strength in the face of damnation. The townsfolk, their despair momentarily lifted, watched with bated breath as the priest confronted the ancient evil that had descended upon their once-peaceful community.

The malevolent vortex, now engaged in a metaphysical battle with the priest, emitted an otherworldly roar. The very ground beneath the town square quivered, and the air became charged with a supernatural tension. Shadows writhed and recoiled as Father Matthias's incantations intensified, forming a barrier that sought to repel the encroaching darkness.

The family and Samuel, still ensnared in the nightmarish dance, faltered in their movements as the divine energy clashed with the malevolent forces that guided them. The spectral figure, its form wavering within the vortex, observed the unfolding struggle with an intensity that mirrored the ancient prophecies.

As the battle between light and darkness reached its zenith, an unearthly scream echoed through the town square. The malevolent vortex, wounded by the radiant power of the crucifix, convulsed with an unholy fury. Judas Iscariot, his form flickering like a fading shadow, retreated into the shadows, vowing a malevolent reprisal.

Father Matthias, his strength bolstered by an unwavering faith, stood at the center of the town square, the crucifix held high. The townsfolk, their spirits lifted by the priest's defiance, felt a glimmer of hope pierce through the darkness that had settled over their once-innocent community.

However, the malevolent vortex, though momentarily repelled, remained a looming presence. The town, now scarred by the supernatural onslaught, stood at the precipice of an unending night. The family and Samuel, freed from the immediate grip of the malevolent forces, stood in the town square, their vacant eyes reflecting a lingering influence that refused to fully relinquish its hold.

The spectral figure, though wounded, watched from the shadows, its purpose seemingly unfulfilled. The air crackled with an unnatural stillness, and the townsfolk, while grateful for the reprieve, knew that the ancient evil had only been momentarily thwarted.

Father Matthias, his eyes still vigilant, addressed the townsfolk with a voice that resonated with a sense of urgency. "The battle is not yet won," he declared. "The forces of darkness may retreat, but they shall return unless we uncover the root of this malevolence and eradicate it once and for all."

The townsfolk, now united in their shared plight, looked towards the abandoned mansion—the epicenter of the supernatural maelstrom that had befallen their community. The spectral figure, though wounded, seemed to beckon them towards the foreboding estate, hinting at the untold secrets that lay within its haunted halls.

As the townsfolk gathered their courage, Father Matthias led the way towards the mansion, crucifix in hand. The malevolent vortex, wounded but not defeated, lingered in the shadows, its echoes of damnation reverberating through the town square.

The once-quiet town, now scarred by the supernatural onslaught, stood at the crossroads of damnation and redemption. The abandoned mansion, its halls echoing with untold secrets, awaited the arrival of those brave enough to unveil the truth that lay hidden within its forsaken walls.

Chapter 9: The Haunting Labyrinth - Unraveling the Dark Tapestry

The townsfolk, guided by Father Matthias, approached the looming mansion with trepidation. The air around the ancient estate seemed to hum with an otherworldly energy, and the shadows clung to its dilapidated walls like whispers of forgotten torment.

As they crossed the threshold, a cold breeze swept through the grand foyer, carrying with it the echoes of centuries-old secrets. The abandoned mansion, now a bastion of malevolence, stood as a silent witness to the supernatural forces that had been unleashed upon the town.

Father Matthias led the way, his crucifix held high as a beacon against the encroaching darkness. The townsfolk followed closely, their faces etched with a mixture of fear and determination. The grand staircase beckoned like a portal to the unknown, and the air seemed to thicken as they ascended towards the upper floors.

In the dimly lit hallways, the spectral figure that had guided Samuel Green lingered, its form wavering between shadows. The wounds inflicted by the priest's radiant power had left the figure weakened, yet an air of malevolence clung to its presence. It observed the procession with an intensity that hinted at an agenda hidden within the tapestry of darkness.

The family and Samuel, still under the lingering influence of the malevolent forces, moved with an unnatural grace. Their vacant eyes betrayed a struggle between the remnants of their humanity and the insidious whispers that sought to bind them to the dark prophecy.

As the group explored the mansion's upper floors, the air became charged with an ominous tension. Unseen whispers echoed through the halls, carrying tales of forbidden rituals and ancient curses. The very walls seemed to bear witness to the supernatural drama that had unfolded within their confines.

Father Matthias, his senses attuned to the malevolence that lingered within the mansion, guided the group towards a forgotten study—the very room where Samuel had unearthed the ancient manuscripts that revealed the dark history of the town.

In the study, the air seemed to crackle with an unearthly energy. The forgotten manuscripts lay scattered across the dusty shelves, their fragile pages seemingly alive with an unholy fervor. The crucifix in Father Matthias's hand emitted a soft glow, casting a circle of light within the dimly lit room.

As the townsfolk gathered around, Father Matthias began to decipher the ancient texts. The words, written in a language that transcended mortal understanding, revealed the origins of the cursed mansion and the malevolent forces that had long sought to return from the depths of Hell.

The tale spoke of a cult that had worshipped dark entities and sought forbidden knowledge. The cult's rituals, conducted within the very mansion that now loomed over the townsfolk, had awakened an ancient evil—an entity with the power to manipulate the fabric of reality itself.

Judas Iscariot, the puppeteer of damnation, had been drawn to the cult's rituals. The cultists, blinded by their pursuit of power, had unwittingly become pawns in a supernatural game that transcended the boundaries of time and space. The thirty pieces of silver, infused with demonic power, served as conduits for the malevolent force—an essence that sought to wreak havoc upon the mortal realm.

As Father Matthias delved deeper into the texts, a revelation unfolded—a prophecy that foretold the return of Judas Iscariot through a vessel chosen by the forces of darkness. The unwitting touch of the ancient coins had initiated a dance of possession, where the boundaries between the living and the damned blurred into a nightmarish tableau.

The townsfolk, their faces pale with realization, listened in silence as Father Matthias spoke of the only way to break the curse—to find and destroy the thirty pieces of silver that had become conduits for the malevolent force. The spectral figure, lingering in the shadows, seemed to shudder at the prospect, hinting at the ancient power that bound it to the mansion's haunted halls.

With newfound purpose, the townsfolk and Father Matthias embarked on a journey through the mansion, guided by the ancient texts. The grand estate, now a labyrinth of forgotten torment, seemed to shift and contort as if responding to the group's quest to unveil the truth.

The family and Samuel, caught in the ebb and flow of the supernatural currents, followed the procession with vacant eyes. The malevolent forces that bound them to the dark prophecy whispered in their minds, urging them to resist the path of redemption.

As the group explored the mansion's hidden chambers and forgotten alcoves, the air became heavy with a sense of foreboding. The very walls seemed to pulse with an ancient malevolence, and the shadows coalesced into grotesque shapes that mocked the living.

In a hidden chamber deep within the mansion, the group discovered an ancient altar adorned with cryptic symbols. On the altar lay a single ancient coin—the very coin that had initiated the nightmarish dance. The air in the chamber hummed with an unnatural energy, and the shadows seemed to writhe in anticipation.

Father Matthias, guided by an unwavering faith, approached the altar with caution. The crucifix in his hand emitted a radiant glow, pushing back the encroaching darkness. The townsfolk, their hearts heavy with the weight of the ancient curse, watched as the priest prepared to confront the malevolent force that had taken root within the very heart of the mansion.

As Father Matthias raised the crucifix, a surge of dark energy emanated from the ancient coin. The spectral figure, still lingering in the shadows, seemed to recoil as if in pain. The air crackled with an otherworldly tension, and the very fabric of reality seemed to quiver in response to the impending confrontation.

The malevolent force, now fully aware of the group's quest to break the curse, sought to resist the priest's efforts. Shadows converged upon the altar, forming a grotesque silhouette that seemed to defy the laws of nature. Whispers echoed in the chamber, carrying tales of damnation and an ancient power that would not yield easily.

Chapter 10: The Abyssal Confrontation - Battleground of Shadows

As Father Matthias confronted the malevolent force within the hidden chamber, the very air vibrated with an otherworldly tension. The townsfolk, their eyes wide with a mixture of fear and determination, watched as the priest raised the crucifix high, its radiant glow pushing back the encroaching shadows.

The malevolent force, angered by the intrusion, sought to resist the priest's efforts. The ancient coin on the altar pulsed with dark energy, and the shadows coalesced into a spectral figure—a manifestation of the malevolence that sought release. The air crackled with an infernal power as the forces of light and darkness clashed within the confined space of the hidden chamber.

Father Matthias, undeterred by the malevolent presence, began chanting ancient incantations—a barrage of holy words that sought to banish the darkness that had taken root within the mansion. The crucifix in his hand emitted a blinding light, forming a barrier that repelled the encroaching shadows.

The townsfolk, their hearts pounding in their chests, felt a surge of hope as the priest's incantations echoed through the chamber. The family and Samuel, caught in the ebb and flow of the supernatural currents, seemed momentarily freed from the malevolent forces that bound them.

However, the spectral figure, though wounded, emerged from the shadows with renewed intensity. Its form contorted and shifted, mirroring the ancient power that bound it to the mansion. The air within the chamber pulsed with an unholy energy, and the very walls seemed to bleed with the essence of damnation.

"You cannot banish what is destined to return," the spectral figure intoned, its voice echoing through the hidden chamber. "The ancient prophecy has set in motion forces that transcend the feeble boundaries of mortal faith."

Father Matthias, his eyes ablaze with a righteous fervor, continued his incantations, each word a spiritual weapon aimed at the heart of the malevolent force. The townsfolk, caught in the midst of the supernatural battleground, braced themselves for the impending confrontation between light and darkness.

As the priest's incantations reached a crescendo, the ancient coin on the altar emitted a piercing scream—an unnatural sound that seemed to pierce through the very fabric of reality. The spectral figure convulsed, its form flickering like a dying ember, yet an indomitable malevolence clung to its presence.

The family and Samuel, freed from the immediate influence of the malevolent forces, stood at the periphery of the supernatural struggle. Their vacant eyes reflected a glimmer of recognition, a spark of humanity that sought to break through the shadows that still lingered within their souls.

The hidden chamber, now a battleground between the forces of light and darkness, quivered under the strain of the ancient confrontation. The air crackled with an infernal energy, and the walls seemed to pulse with the echoes of centuries-old torment.

In a desperate attempt to thwart the priest's efforts, the spectral figure extended its shadowy tendrils towards the ancient coin. The malevolent force, now fully unleashed, sought to draw upon the demonic power within the coin to repel the encroaching light.

Father Matthias, sensing the malevolent force's desperation, intensified his incantations. The crucifix in his hand emitted a blinding radiance, forming a protective barrier that held back the spectral figure's advance. The very air within the chamber vibrated with the clash of opposing forces—an unholy symphony that echoed through the haunted halls of the mansion.

The townsfolk, their senses assaulted by the supernatural struggle, felt a surge of conflicting energies that seemed to tug at their very souls. The family and Samuel, standing on the fringes of the confrontation, clutched their heads as if trying to resist the unseen currents that sought to ensnare them once more.

As the battle within the hidden chamber reached its zenith, a blinding flash of light erupted from the crucifix. The spectral figure, unable to withstand the divine power, recoiled with a haunting wail. Shadows writhed and contorted, forming grotesque shapes that seemed to dissipate like smoke in the presence of the radiant onslaught.

The ancient coin, stripped of its demonic power, clattered to the floor. The malevolent force, now weakened and wounded, retreated into the shadows, its spectral form flickering like a dying ember. The hidden chamber, once a crucible of supernatural struggle, fell into an eerie stillness as the echoes of the confrontation lingered in the air.

Father Matthias, his strength tested by the supernatural battle, stood at the center of the chamber, the crucifix still held high. The townsfolk, their faces etched with a mixture of relief and awe, approached the priest with newfound reverence. The family and Samuel, released from the immediate grip of the malevolent forces, seemed to regain a semblance of awareness.

"The battle is won, but the war is far from over," Father Matthias declared, his voice carrying the weight of ancient wisdom. "The malevolent force may retreat, but it will seek to return unless we uncover the roots of the curse and eradicate them."

The spectral figure, though wounded and weakened, lingered in the shadows. Its eyes, pools of emptiness, reflected a lingering malevolence that seemed to defy the priest's triumph. The air within the chamber remained charged with an unnatural stillness, hinting at the ancient power that still clung to the mansion's haunted halls.

Guided by the knowledge within the ancient texts, Father Matthias led the townsfolk and the now-aware family and Samuel through the mansion's labyrinthine corridors. The malevolent force, though momentarily subdued, lingered in the shadows, a specter of damnation that awaited an opportune moment to strike once more.

As the group delved deeper into the mansion's secrets, they uncovered hidden chambers and forgotten passages—each revealing a piece of the dark tapestry that had ensnared the town for centuries. Whispers echoed through the haunted halls, carrying tales of forbidden rituals and unspeakable horrors that lurked in the shadows.

The family and Samuel, now cognizant of the malevolent forces that had manipulated them, struggled to resist the lingering whispers that sought to pull them back into the nightmarish dance. The townsfolk, guided by Father Matthias, remained vigilant as they sought to uncover the truth that lay hidden within the mansion's forsaken walls.

In a long-forgotten chamber, adorned with cryptic symbols and ancient relics, the group discovered a series of ancient artifacts—each linked to the malevolent forces that had plagued the town. The artifacts, imbued with dark energy, seemed to resonate with the lingering malevolence that clung to the mansion's haunted halls.

Father Matthias, his eyes gleaming with a sense of revelation, identified the artifacts as keys to the curse that bound the town. The family and Samuel, now aware of their roles in the ancient prophecy, looked upon the artifacts with a mixture of dread and determination.

The townsfolk, united in their quest for redemption, prepared to embark on a perilous journey—a journey that would take them beyond the boundaries of the mansion and into the depths of Hell itself. The spectral figure, though weakened, watched from the shadows, its purpose seemingly unfulfilled.

As the group descended into the mansion's subterranean depths, the air became heavy with the stench of ancient malevolence. The walls seemed to close in, and the shadows writhed with an eerie anticipation. The journey into the abyss had just begun, and the fate of the town hung in the balance as the group delved further into the darkness that had ensnared them all.

Chapter 11: Descent into the Abyss - Echoes of Damnation

The subterranean depths of the mansion unfurled like a labyrinthine nightmare, each corridor a passage into the ancient malevolence that lurked beneath. Father Matthias, clutching the crucifix with unwavering resolve, led the townsfolk and the now-aware family and Samuel into the abyss. The air became thick with an ominous energy, and the walls seemed to close in as if bearing witness to the trespassers who sought to unravel the curse that bound the town.

The spectral figure, though weakened, trailed behind like a lingering shadow. Its form contorted and shifted, mirroring the malevolent forces that still clung to the mansion's haunted halls. The air within the subterranean depths hummed with an unnatural resonance, and the very ground seemed to pulse with echoes of centuries-old torment.

As the group navigated through the winding passages, ancient whispers echoed through the darkness—tales of forbidden rituals, unspeakable horrors, and the malevolent entities that lurked in the abyss. The family and Samuel, now aware of the weight of their unwitting involvement in the ancient prophecy, struggled to resist the siren call of the shadows that sought to ensnare them once more.

The artifacts, discovered in the hidden chamber, served as keys to unlock the cursed seal that bound the town. Father Matthias, guided by the ancient texts, led the group towards a foreboding chamber—a gateway to the depths of Hell itself. The very air within the chamber seemed to writhe with infernal energy, and the walls bore symbols that hinted at an ancient power waiting to be unleashed.

Ethan, Emma, and Lily, their eyes reflecting a lingering influence, followed the group with an eerie grace. Samuel, burdened by the weight of the malevolent forces that had possessed him, walked with a haunted determination. The townsfolk, their faces etched with a mixture of fear and determination, looked towards Father Matthias for guidance in the face of the impending descent into darkness.

As the group entered the chamber, the air crackled with an otherworldly tension. The symbols on the walls seemed to come alive, pulsating with an ancient power that resonated with the very essence of damnation. Father Matthias, his senses attuned to the supernatural currents, approached the center of the chamber where an ancient altar stood.

On the altar lay the artifacts, each exuding a malevolent energy that seemed to respond to the presence of the group. Father Matthias, with a solemn determination, began arranging the artifacts in a pattern that echoed the ancient texts—a pattern that served as a key to unlock the curse that bound the town.

The spectral figure, though weakened, observed the unfolding ritual with a malevolent intensity. The air within the chamber became charged with an unnatural stillness, and the shadows seemed to gather around the group as if awaiting the moment when the ancient forces would be set free.

Father Matthias, his incantations resonating with the echoes of centuries-old prophecies, raised the crucifix high. The artifacts, arranged in a precise configuration, emitted a malevolent glow that bathed the chamber in an eerie light. The very ground beneath the group seemed to quiver as the ritual reached its zenith.

Suddenly, the air within the chamber vibrated with an otherworldly resonance. The walls shook, and the symbols etched upon them seemed to writhe in anticipation. Whispers echoed through the chamber, carrying tales of ancient entities and the impending descent into the depths of Hell.

Ethan, Emma, and Lily, their vacant eyes reflecting the malevolent glow, stood at the periphery of the ritual. Samuel, his body a vessel for the forces that sought release, trembled as the ancient power surged through his veins. The townsfolk, caught in the midst of the supernatural spectacle, braced themselves for the unknown as the ancient seal began to unravel.

The spectral figure, its form wavering within the shadows, seemed to shudder as if in pain. The artifacts, now imbued with the malevolent energy, emitted a collective hum that resonated with the very fabric of reality. The air crackled with infernal power, and the subterranean depths of the mansion became a battleground where the forces of light and darkness clashed with a ferocity that transcended mortal understanding.

As the ritual reached its climax, a portal began to materialize at the center of the chamber—a gateway to the depths of Hell itself. The air within the portal shimmered with an infernal glow, and the very walls seemed to bleed with the essence of damnation. The townsfolk, their faces etched with horror, watched as the ancient forces sought release through the newfound gateway.

Father Matthias, his eyes ablaze with a righteous fervor, continued his incantations, seeking to maintain control over the supernatural maelstrom that threatened to engulf the group. The spectral figure, now fully entwined with the shadows, emitted a haunting wail as if resisting the impending liberation of the malevolent forces.

Ethan, Emma, and Lily, their bodies now mere vessels for the ancient entities, approached the gateway with an eerie grace. Samuel, caught in the ebb and flow of the supernatural currents, moved with a haunted determination as if compelled by an unseen force. The townsfolk, their hearts pounding in their chests, stood at the precipice of an unending night.

As the portal to Hell widened, a figure emerged—a manifestation of the ancient entities that sought release. The entity, shrouded in darkness, bore a twisted visage that mirrored the very shadows that danced within the depths of the abyss. The air within the chamber quivered as the entity, an emissary of the malevolent forces, surveyed the group with eyes that burned with an unholy intensity.

"The time has come," the entity declared, its voice echoing through the chamber. "The prophecy unfolds, and Hell itself shall walk among the living."

The townsfolk, their senses assaulted by the malevolent presence, felt a surge of despair settle over them. The family and Samuel, now mere puppets in the hands of the ancient entities, stood at the forefront of the unfolding nightmare. The spectral figure, its purpose seemingly unfulfilled, watched with a malevolent satisfaction as the gateway to Hell yawned wide.

Father Matthias, undeterred by the impending darkness, raised the crucifix high and continued his incantations. The artifacts, now arranged in the pattern dictated by the ancient texts, emitted a radiant glow that pushed back the encroaching shadows. The very fabric of reality seemed to shudder as the forces of light and darkness clashed in a supernatural struggle that transcended the boundaries of mortal understanding.

As the entity from the depths of Hell extended its shadowy tendrils towards the group, Father Matthias invoked the divine forces with unwavering faith. The townsfolk, their hearts heavy with the weight of an impending doom, braced themselves for the final confrontation that would determine the fate of the town.

In the midst of the supernatural maelstrom, a voice echoed through the chamber—a voice that seemed to cut through the infernal cacophony. The spectral figure, though weakened, spoke with a resonance that carried the weight of forgotten prophecies.

"The true power lies not in the gateway, but in the choices made within the abyss," the spectral figure intoned, its voice a haunting melody amidst the chaos. "Redemption or damnation, the path is yours to choose."

The townsfolk, caught in the grip of an otherworldly struggle, listened to the spectral figure's words with a sense of revelation. Father Matthias, his faith unwavering, continued his incantations, seeking to seal the gateway and banish the malevolent entity back to the depths of Hell.

Ethan, Emma, and Lily, their vacant eyes reflecting a lingering humanity, stood at the crossroads of redemption and damnation. Samuel, burdened by the malevolent forces that had possessed him, seemed to waver between the forces that sought control.

The entity from the depths of Hell, now fully manifested, roared with an infernal fury as the radiant power of the crucifix pushed back its shadowy tendrils. The very walls of the chamber seemed to tremble as the forces of light and darkness engaged in a final, cataclysmic struggle.

The townsfolk, their destinies hanging in the balance, faced a choice that would shape the fate of the town. The family and Samuel, still caught in the grip of the ancient prophecy, stood at the forefront of the supernatural battleground. The spectral figure, its form flickering within the shadows, observed the unfolding drama with an intensity that mirrored the ancient prophecies that had set the stage for the nightmarish ordeal.

As the chamber quivered under the strain of the supernatural struggle, the townsfolk, guided by their own choices, prepared to face the abyss that awaited them. The air crackled with an unnatural tension, and the very fabric of reality seemed to warp as the forces of light and darkness clashed in a final, climactic confrontation. The fate of the town, now hanging in the balance, awaited the resolution of the choices made within the depths of the abyss.

Chapter 12: The Abyssal Choice - Redemption or Damnation

The subterranean chamber quivered under the strain of the supernatural struggle between light and darkness. The gateway to Hell, wide open and pulsating with infernal energy, cast a ghastly glow that bathed the surroundings in an eerie light. The townsfolk, caught in the grip of an otherworldly confrontation, faced a choice that would shape the very fabric of their existence.

Father Matthias, undeterred by the looming malevolence, continued his incantations. The crucifix in his hand emitted a radiant glow that pushed back the encroaching shadows. The artifacts, arranged in a pattern dictated by ancient prophecies, resonated with a divine power that sought to seal the gateway and banish the entity from the depths of Hell.

Ethan, Emma, and Lily, their vacant eyes reflecting a glimmer of recognition, stood at the forefront of the supernatural battleground. Samuel, burdened by the malevolent forces that had possessed him, wavered between the forces that sought control. The family and Samuel, now aware of the choices that awaited them, stood at the crossroads of redemption and damnation.

The entity from the depths of Hell, fully manifested and roiling with infernal fury, extended its shadowy tendrils towards the group. The air within the chamber vibrated with an otherworldly resonance as the forces of light and darkness clashed in a final, cataclysmic confrontation.

"The time for choices has come," the spectral figure intoned, its voice echoing through the chamber. "Redemption or damnation, the path is yours to choose."

The townsfolk, their hearts heavy with fear prayed aloud.

Chapter 12: The Abyssal Choice - Redemption or Damnation

The subterranean chamber quivered under the strain of the supernatural struggle between light and darkness. The gateway to Hell, wide open and pulsating with infernal energy, cast a ghastly glow that bathed the surroundings in an eerie light. The townsfolk, caught in the grip of an otherworldly confrontation, faced a choice that would shape the very fabric of their existence.

Father Matthias, undeterred by the looming malevolence, continued his incantations. The crucifix in his hand emitted a radiant glow that pushed back the encroaching shadows. The artifacts, arranged in a pattern dictated by ancient prophecies, resonated with a divine power that sought to seal the gateway and banish the entity from the depths of Hell.

Ethan, Emma, and Lily, their vacant eyes reflecting a glimmer of recognition, stood at the forefront of the supernatural battleground. Samuel, burdened by the malevolent forces that had possessed him, wavered between the forces that sought control. The family and Samuel, now aware of the choices that awaited them, stood at the crossroads of redemption and damnation.

The entity from the depths of Hell, fully manifested and roiling with infernal fury, extended its shadowy tendrils towards the group. The air within the chamber vibrated with an otherworldly resonance as the forces of light and darkness clashed in a final, cataclysmic confrontation.

"The time for choices has come," the spectral figure intoned, its voice echoing through the chamber. "Redemption or damnation, the path is yours to choose."

The townsfolk, their hearts heavy with the weight of impending doom, felt the very air quiver with the supernatural forces that surrounded them. The family and Samuel, now aware of the magnitude of the choices before them, stood as reluctant protagonists in a nightmarish drama that had unfolded through the annals of time.

Ethan, Emma, and Lily, their humanity struggling to break free from the malevolent forces that bound them, exchanged glances that spoke of shared fear and determination. Samuel, caught in the throes of the ancient prophecy, fought against the insidious whispers that sought to manipulate his every thought.

Father Matthias, his eyes ablaze with a fervent faith, raised the crucifix higher. The artifacts on the ancient altar emitted a divine glow that pulsated in rhythm with the priest's incantations. The very ground beneath the group seemed to shudder as the supernatural confrontation reached its zenith.

The entity from the depths of Hell, its form a grotesque silhouette against the pulsating gateway, roared with an infernal fury. The shadows writhed and contorted, forming a grotesque tableau that seemed to defy the laws of nature. The air within the chamber crackled with an unholy energy, and the very walls seemed to bleed with the essence of damnation.

As the malevolent entity extended its shadowy tendrils towards the family and Samuel, a chorus of ancient whispers echoed through the chamber. Each whisper carried tales of redemption and damnation, weaving a tapestry of choices that transcended the mortal realm. The townsfolk, standing at the crossroads of destiny, felt the weight of their choices bear down upon them like an impending storm.

Ethan, Emma, and Lily, their eyes now flickering with a glimmer of resistance, hesitated at the precipice of the abyss. Samuel, his will caught in the tug-of-war between the forces that sought to possess him, struggled against the unseen chains that bound him to the ancient prophecy.

Father Matthias, his voice resonating with a divine power, addressed the family and Samuel with a solemn urgency. "The choices you make within this abyss will echo through the corridors of time. The forces of darkness seek to ensnare, but redemption is a beacon that can guide you out of the shadows."

The townsfolk, caught in the supernatural maelstrom, listened to the priest's words with a sense of hope and trepidation. The spectral figure, though weakened, observed the unfolding drama with an intensity that hinted at an ancient power still lingering within the shadows.

Ethan, Emma, and Lily, their inner struggles etched on their faces, faced the gateway with a collective hesitation. The malevolent forces that had held them captive seemed to recoil in the face of their wavering resolve. Samuel, caught between the forces of redemption and damnation, stood as a tragic figure in the cosmic play that unfolded within the subterranean chamber.

As the entity from the depths of Hell roared with an infernal fury, the family and Samuel, guided by an inner strength, took a collective step away from the malevolent gateway. The air within the chamber seemed to ripple with an unseen force as the choices made by each individual resonated through the supernatural currents that bound them.

The spectral figure, its form flickering within the shadows, spoke with a voice that carried the weight of forgotten prophecies. "The abyss may be a test, but the choices made within its depths have the power to shape destinies. Beware, for the forces that seek your damnation will not yield easily."

Father Matthias, sensing the momentous nature of the choices made, continued his incantations with an unwavering determination. The crucifix in his hand emitted a radiant glow that served as a barrier against the encroaching shadows. The artifacts, arranged in a pattern that mirrored the choices made by the family and Samuel, resonated with a divine power that sought to seal the malevolent gateway.

The entity from the depths of Hell, now facing the resistance of those standing at the crossroads, writhed with an otherworldly anguish. The shadows seemed to recoil, and the very fabric of the malevolent force quivered in response to the choices made by the family and Samuel.

Ethan, Emma, and Lily, their faces now reflecting a glimmer of defiance, stepped further away from the gateway. The malevolent forces that had ensnared them seemed to lose their grip, their influence diminishing as the choices of redemption echoed through the abyss.

Samuel, caught in the struggle for his own soul, hesitated. The malevolent forces whispered promises of power and ancient knowledge, tempting him to embrace the darkness that sought to consume him. The family, their eyes now focused on Samuel, exchanged glances that spoke of a shared hope for his redemption.

Father Matthias, sensing the pivotal moment, directed his incantations towards Samuel. The crucifix in his hand emitted a radiant glow that reached out like a beacon, seeking to pierce through the shadows that bound Samuel to the ancient prophecy.

As the entity from the depths of Hell roared with an infernal fury, Samuel, torn between the forces of light and darkness, took a hesitant step away from the malevolent gateway. The air within the chamber seemed to ripple with a sense of cosmic significance as the choices made within the abyss echoed through the haunted halls of the mansion.

The spectral figure, its form flickering within the shadows, spoke with a voice that carried the weight of an ancient wisdom. "Choices made in the face of damnation can become the keys to redemption. The true test lies in the resilience of the human spirit."

The entity, now facing a collective resistance, recoiled with an otherworldly scream. The shadows seemed to dissipate, and the malevolent forces that had sought release through the gateway faltered in the face of the choices made by the family and Samuel.

The townsfolk, their senses attuned to the supernatural currents that surrounded them, felt a surge of relief as the malevolent forces retreated. The gateway to Hell, once wide open and pulsating with infernal energy, began to close, its ethereal glow dimming as the forces of light regained control.

Father Matthias, his voice carrying a sense of triumph, completed the incantations. The artifacts on the ancient altar resonated with a divine power that sealed the malevolent gateway. The very air within the chamber seemed to sigh with the release of tension, and the shadows that had clung to the walls dissipated like smoke in the wake of a vanquishing storm.

The family and Samuel, now free from the immediate influence of the malevolent forces, stood in the aftermath of the supernatural confrontation. The townsfolk, their faces etched with a mixture of awe and relief, approached the group with a newfound reverence.

"The choices you made within the abyss were not just yours but resonated with the very fabric of existence," Father Matthias declared, his eyes gleaming with a profound wisdom. "The forces of darkness may seek to entrap, but the human spirit, guided by choices of redemption, can triumph over even the deepest abyss."

The spectral figure, its form flickering within the shadows, spoke with a voice that seemed to carry a sense of finality. "The gateway may be sealed, but the echoes of the abyss will linger. Beware, for the malevolent forces may seek another path to release."

As the townsfolk absorbed the gravity of the moment, the family and Samuel, now free from the immediate grip of the malevolent forces, exchanged glances that spoke of shared trauma and newfound resilience. The spectral figure, its purpose seemingly fulfilled, faded into the shadows, leaving behind an eerie stillness within the subterranean chamber.

Father Matthias, sensing that the true roots of the curse still lay hidden within the mansion, turned his attention towards the family and Samuel. "The journey is not over. The malevolent forces may retreat, but the shadows that linger within the mansion hold secrets that must be revealed."

The family and Samuel, now aware of the ongoing battle against the ancient curse, nodded with a shared determination. The townsfolk, their faces etched with gratitude, looked towards Father Matthias as a beacon of hope in the midst of the supernatural darkness.

The subterranean chamber, once a battleground of shadows, fell into an eerie stillness. The artifacts on the ancient altar, now dormant but still resonating with a divine power, served as a reminder of the choices made within the abyss. The gateway to Hell, sealed by the collective will of those standing at the crossroads, faded into a mere memory within the haunted halls of the mansion.

As the group prepared to leave the subterranean depths, the air seemed lighter, and the very walls of the chamber appeared to exhale a sigh of relief. The journey to uncover the secrets that lay hidden within the mansion had just begun, and the family and Samuel, guided by Father Matthias and the collective will of the townsfolk, faced a path that led into the heart of the curse that had plagued the town for centuries.

The haunted mansion, its halls echoing with the remnants of the supernatural confrontation, awaited the revelation of the ancient truths that had been concealed within its forsaken walls. The family and Samuel, now united in their quest for redemption, stepped out of the subterranean chamber and into the labyrinthine corridors of the mansion, where the shadows still clung to the secrets that had yet to be unveiled.

Chapter 13: Shadows Unveiled - The Mansion's Ancient Secrets

The labyrinthine corridors of the haunted mansion stretched like a nightmarish maze, each step echoing with the weight of centuries-old secrets. Father Matthias led the family and Samuel through the dimly lit halls, the air heavy with a palpable tension. The townsfolk, now united in their quest for redemption, followed with a wary determination.

As they traversed the mansion's hidden passages, the walls seemed to close in, shadows dancing with an otherworldly life. The family, their recent brush with damnation etched in their minds, exchanged glances that spoke of shared fear and resilience. Samuel, still haunted by the malevolent forces that had possessed him, walked with a haunted determination.

Father Matthias, his eyes scanning the arcane symbols and cryptic inscriptions that adorned the walls, led the group towards a long-forgotten chamber—the heart of the mansion's ancient secrets. The air within the chamber seemed to pulse with a suppressed energy, and the very walls whispered tales of forbidden knowledge and unspeakable horrors.

The family and Samuel, now aware of the malevolent forces that lurked within the mansion, felt a surge of trepidation as they entered the chamber. Father Matthias, guided by the ancient texts, approached an altar adorned with occult symbols and mysterious artifacts. The townsfolk, their senses on high alert, braced themselves for the revelations that awaited them.

As Father Matthias examined the artifacts, each pulsating with a dormant power, a shiver ran down the collective spine of the group. The spectral figure, though seemingly subdued, lingered within the shadows, its presence a constant reminder of the malevolent forces that had plagued the town for centuries.

"These artifacts hold the key to unraveling the curse that binds this town," Father Matthias proclaimed, his voice carrying the weight of an ancient wisdom. "But to unlock their secrets, we must confront the very origins of the darkness that has infested these walls."

The family and Samuel, now united in their quest for redemption, looked towards Father Matthias with a mixture of hope and trepidation. The artifacts on the altar seemed to pulse with an otherworldly resonance, as if eager to divulge the secrets that had been hidden for generations.

The townsfolk, their faces etched with a mixture of fear and determination, surrounded the altar, ready to face the revelations that awaited them. The spectral figure, its form flickering within the shadows, observed the unfolding drama with an intensity that mirrored the ancient prophecies that had set the stage for the nightmarish ordeal.

Father Matthias, guided by the knowledge within the ancient texts, began to chant incantations that invoked the spirits of the past. The artifacts on the altar responded, emitting a dim glow that seemed to pierce through the veil of time. The air within the chamber quivered as the group became enveloped in an otherworldly aura.

As the incantations reached a crescendo, the walls of the chamber seemed to ripple with an unseen force. Whispers echoed through the air, carrying tales of forbidden rituals and unspeakable pacts that had been made within the mansion's forsaken halls. The family and Samuel, caught in the currents of ancient knowledge, felt the weight of the revelations that surged through the chamber.

Suddenly, the artifacts on the altar emitted a blinding light, and the very air crackled with an infernal energy. The spectral figure, though weakened, writhed within the shadows as if resisting the unveiling of the secrets that had been concealed for centuries. The townsfolk, their eyes wide with a mixture of awe and fear, braced themselves for the revelations that awaited them.

The chamber, now bathed in an ethereal glow, seemed to transcend the boundaries of time. Visions of the past flickered within the light—shadows of long-forgotten rituals, echoes of tormented souls, and the malevolent forces that had manipulated the destinies of those who had crossed the mansion's threshold.

Ethan, Emma, and Lily, their eyes reflecting the flickering visions, witnessed glimpses of their own ancestors entangled in a cosmic dance with ancient entities. Samuel, his connection to the ancient prophecy now laid bare, saw fragments of the choices that had shaped the destiny of the town.

Father Matthias, undeterred by the supernatural revelations, continued his incantations, seeking to unravel the ancient tapestry that bound the mansion in a web of darkness. The artifacts on the altar, now pulsating with an otherworldly energy, seemed to resonate with the very fabric of reality.

As the visions reached their zenith, a voice echoed through the chamber—a voice that seemed to transcend time itself. The spectral figure, now fully entwined with the shadows, spoke with a resonance that carried the weight of forgotten prophecies.

"The mansion is a vessel of ancient power, a gateway between the mortal realm and the shadows that linger beyond," the spectral figure intoned, its voice echoing through the chamber. "The curse that plagues this town is a consequence of choices made within its walls, choices that bind the living and the dead in an eternal dance of torment."

The townsfolk, their senses assaulted by the revelations, listened to the spectral figure's words with a sense of awe and dread. The family and Samuel, now cognizant of the ancient forces that had manipulated the destinies of their ancestors, stood at the precipice of an abyss that threatened to swallow them whole.

As the visions subsided, the chamber returned to a dimly lit reality. The artifacts on the altar, though still pulsating with a dormant power, no longer emitted the blinding light that had revealed the secrets of the past. The family and Samuel, their minds reeling from the cosmic revelations, exchanged glances that spoke of a shared understanding.

Father Matthias, his eyes gleaming with a profound wisdom, addressed the group with a solemn urgency. "The mansion is a nexus of ancient power, a conduit through which the malevolent forces have sought to manipulate the destinies of those who dwell within its walls. But the choices we make now can shape a different fate for this town."

The townsfolk, now burdened with the knowledge of the mansion's dark history, looked towards Father Matthias with a sense of determination. The spectral figure, though weakened, observed the group with an intensity that hinted at the lingering malevolence that still clung to the mansion's haunted halls.

"The artifacts hold the key to breaking the curse, but their power must be harnessed with care," Father Matthias continued. "We must delve further into the mansion's secrets, confront the shadows that linger within, and uncover the true source of the curse that has plagued this town for centuries."

The family and Samuel, now united with the townsfolk in a shared quest for redemption, nodded with a collective resolve. The ancient artifacts, still pulsating with a dormant power, seemed to resonate with the determination of those who sought to break the shackles of the curse.

The group, guided by Father Matthias and armed with the knowledge of the mansion's ancient secrets, ventured deeper into the labyrinthine corridors. The spectral figure, its form flickering within the shadows, followed with a watchful gaze, its purpose seemingly entwined with the unfolding drama.

As they navigated through the haunted halls, the air seemed to thicken with an otherworldly energy. The walls whispered tales of forgotten rituals and unspeakable pacts that had left an indelible mark on the mansion's tortured history. The family and Samuel, now aware of the choices that awaited them, walked with a collective determination that echoed through the forsaken halls.

The mansion, once a bastion of shadows and secrets, awaited the revelation of the true source of the curse. The artifacts, now in the possession of those who sought redemption, held the key to unlocking the ancient power that had bound the town in a cycle of torment. The spectral figure, its purpose yet to be fully understood, lingered within the shadows, a silent witness to the unfolding quest for salvation.

As the group delved deeper into the heart of the mansion's secrets, the very air seemed to vibrate with an otherworldly tension. The shadows that clung to the walls whispered of the malevolent forces that sought to resist the intrusion of those who sought to break the curse. The family and Samuel, guided by the flickering light of the ancient artifacts, pressed on with a shared determination that defied the darkness that sought to engulf them.

The labyrinthine corridors, once a maze of uncertainty, became a battleground where the forces of light and darkness clashed in a cosmic struggle. The spectral figure, though weakened, observed the unfolding drama with a sense of anticipation, its role in the ancient prophecies still shrouded in mystery.

As the group ventured further into the mansion's depths, the very fabric of reality seemed to warp. The air became heavy with the echoes of forgotten prophecies, and the walls bore witness to the choices made by those who sought to confront the shadows that lingered within. The family and Samuel, now burdened with the weight of their newfound knowledge, stood at the precipice of an abyss that held the key to the town's salvation.

The haunted mansion, its ancient secrets on the verge of being unveiled, awaited the resolution of the quest for redemption. The artifacts, still pulsating with a dormant power, served as beacons that illuminated the path into the heart of the curse. The family and Samuel, guided by Father Matthias and the collective will of the townsfolk, braced themselves for the revelations that awaited them within the shadows that had concealed the mansion's dark history for far too long.

Chapter 13: Shadows Unveiled - The Mansion's Ancient Secrets

The labyrinthine corridors of the haunted mansion stretched like a nightmarish maze, each step echoing with the weight of centuries-old secrets. Father Matthias led the family and Samuel through the dimly lit halls, the air heavy with a palpable tension. The townsfolk, now united in their quest for redemption, followed with a wary determination.

As they traversed the mansion's hidden passages, the walls seemed to close in, shadows dancing with an otherworldly life. The family, their recent brush with damnation etched in their minds, exchanged glances that spoke of shared fear and resilience. Samuel, still haunted by the malevolent forces that had possessed him, walked with a haunted determination.

Father Matthias, his eyes scanning the arcane symbols and cryptic inscriptions that adorned the walls, led the group towards a long-forgotten chamber—the heart of the mansion's ancient secrets. The air within the chamber seemed to pulse with a suppressed energy, and the very walls whispered tales of forbidden knowledge and unspeakable horrors.

The family and Samuel, now aware of the malevolent forces that lurked within the mansion, felt a surge of trepidation as they entered the chamber. Father Matthias, guided by the ancient texts, approached an altar adorned with occult symbols and mysterious artifacts. The townsfolk, their senses on high alert, braced themselves for the revelations that awaited them.

As Father Matthias examined the artifacts, each pulsating with a dormant power, a shiver ran down the collective spine of the group. The spectral figure, though seemingly subdued, lingered within the shadows, its presence a constant reminder of the malevolent forces that had plagued the town for centuries.

"These artifacts hold the key to unraveling the curse that binds this town," Father Matthias proclaimed, his voice carrying the weight of an ancient wisdom. "But to unlock their secrets, we must confront the very origins of the darkness that has infested these walls."

The family and Samuel, now united in their quest for redemption, looked towards Father Matthias with a mixture of hope and trepidation. The artifacts on the altar seemed to pulse with an otherworldly resonance, as if eager to divulge the secrets that had been hidden for generations.

The townsfolk, their faces etched with a mixture of fear and determination, surrounded the altar, ready to face the revelations that awaited them. The spectral figure, though weakened, observed the unfolding drama with an intensity that mirrored the ancient prophecies that had set the stage for the nightmarish ordeal.

Father Matthias, guided by the knowledge within the ancient texts, began to chant incantations that invoked the spirits of the past. The artifacts on the altar responded, emitting a dim glow that seemed to pierce through the veil of time. The air within the chamber quivered as the group became enveloped in an otherworldly aura.

As the incantations reached a crescendo, the walls of the chamber seemed to ripple with an unseen force. Whispers echoed through the air, carrying tales of forbidden rituals and unspeakable pacts that had been made within the mansion's forsaken halls. The family and Samuel, caught in the currents of ancient knowledge, felt the weight of the revelations that surged through the chamber.

Suddenly, the artifacts on the altar emitted a blinding light, and the very air crackled with an infernal energy. The spectral figure, though weakened, writhed within the shadows as if resisting the unveiling of the secrets that had been concealed for centuries. The townsfolk, their eyes wide with a mixture of awe and fear, braced themselves for the revelations that awaited them.

The chamber, now bathed in an ethereal glow, seemed to transcend the boundaries of time. Visions of the past flickered within the light—shadows of long-forgotten rituals, echoes of tormented souls, and the malevolent forces that had manipulated the destinies of those who had crossed the mansion's threshold.

Ethan, Emma, and Lily, their eyes reflecting the flickering visions, witnessed glimpses of their own ancestors entangled in a cosmic dance with ancient entities. Samuel, his connection to the ancient prophecy now laid bare, saw fragments of the choices that had shaped the destiny of the town.

Father Matthias, undeterred by the supernatural revelations, continued his incantations, seeking to unravel the ancient tapestry that bound the mansion in a web of darkness. The artifacts on the altar, now pulsating with an otherworldly energy, seemed to resonate with the very fabric of reality.

As the visions reached their zenith, a voice echoed through the chamber—a voice that seemed to transcend time itself. The spectral figure, now fully entwined with the shadows, spoke with a resonance that carried the weight of forgotten prophecies.

"The mansion is a vessel of ancient power, a gateway between the mortal realm and the shadows that linger beyond," the spectral figure intoned, its voice echoing through the chamber. "The curse that plagues this town is a consequence of choices made within its walls, choices that bind the living and the dead in an eternal dance of torment."

The townsfolk, their senses assaulted by the revelations, listened to the spectral figure's words with a sense of awe and dread. The family and Samuel, now cognizant of the ancient forces that had manipulated the destinies of their ancestors, stood at the precipice of an abyss that threatened to swallow them whole.

As the visions subsided, the chamber returned to a dimly lit reality. The artifacts on the altar, though still pulsating with a dormant power, no longer emitted the blinding light that had revealed the secrets of the past. The family and Samuel, their minds reeling from the cosmic revelations, exchanged glances that spoke of a shared understanding.

Father Matthias, his eyes gleaming with a profound wisdom, addressed the group with a solemn urgency. "The mansion is a nexus of ancient power, a conduit through which the malevolent forces have sought to manipulate the destinies of those who dwell within its walls. But the choices we make now can shape a different fate for this town."

The townsfolk, now burdened with the knowledge of the mansion's dark history, looked towards Father Matthias with a sense of determination. The spectral figure, though weakened, observed the group with an intensity that hinted at the lingering malevolence that still clung to the mansion's haunted halls.

"The artifacts hold the key to breaking the curse, but their power must be harnessed with care," Father Matthias continued. "We must delve further into the mansion's secrets, confront the shadows that linger within, and uncover the true source of the curse that has plagued this town for centuries."

The family and Samuel, now united with the townsfolk in a shared quest for redemption, nodded with a collective resolve. The ancient artifacts, still pulsating with a dormant power, seemed to resonate with the determination of those who sought to break the shackles of the curse.

The group, guided by Father Matthias and armed with the knowledge of the mansion's ancient secrets, ventured deeper into the labyrinthine corridors. The spectral figure, though weakened, followed with a watchful gaze, its purpose seemingly entwined with the unfolding drama.

As they navigated through the haunted halls, the air seemed to thicken with an otherworldly energy. The walls whispered tales of forgotten rituals and unspeakable pacts that had left an indelible mark on the mansion's tortured history. The family and Samuel, now aware of the choices that awaited them, walked with a collective determination that echoed through the forsaken halls.

The mansion, once a bastion of shadows and secrets, awaited the revelation of the true source of the curse. The artifacts, now in the possession of those who sought redemption, held the key to unlocking the ancient power that had bound the town in a cycle of torment. The spectral figure, its purpose yet to be fully understood, lingered within the shadows, a silent witness to the unfolding quest for salvation.

As the group prepared to face the deeper mysteries that lay ahead, the very air within the mansion seemed to hum with an otherworldly resonance. The shadows, though momentarily subdued, whispered of the malevolent forces that still clung to the secrets concealed within the haunted halls. The family and Samuel, guided by the flickering light of the ancient artifacts, pressed on with a shared determination that defied the darkness that sought to engulf them.

The labyrinthine corridors, once a maze of uncertainty, became a battleground where the forces of light and darkness clashed in a cosmic struggle. The spectral figure, though weakened, observed the unfolding drama with a sense of anticipation, its role in the ancient prophecies still shrouded in mystery.

As the group ventured further into the mansion's depths, the very fabric of reality seemed to warp. The air became heavy with the echoes of forgotten prophecies, and the walls bore witness to the choices made by those who sought to confront the shadows that lingered within. The family and Samuel, now burdened with the weight of their newfound knowledge, stood at the precipice of an abyss that held the key to the town's salvation.

The haunted mansion, its ancient secrets on the verge of being unveiled, awaited the resolution of the quest for redemption. The artifacts, still pulsating with a dormant power, served as beacons that illuminated the path into the heart of the curse. The family and Samuel, guided by Father Matthias and the collective will of the townsfolk, braced themselves for the revelations that awaited them within the shadows that had concealed the mansion's dark history for far too long.

Chapter 14: The Lurking Abyss - Unearthing the Dark Covenant

The group ventured deeper into the heart of the mansion, guided by the flickering light of the ancient artifacts and the resolute determination instilled by Father Matthias. The labyrinthine corridors seemed to coil like a serpent, tightening around them with an unsettling embrace. The air grew colder, and the very walls appeared to pulse with a malevolent energy.

As they advanced, the shadows played tricks on their senses—whispers of ethereal voices and fleeting glimpses of spectral figures that vanished as quickly as they appeared. The family and Samuel, now attuned to the supernatural currents, walked on the precipice of a nightmare, their resolve tested with every echoing footstep.

Father Matthias, the bearer of ancient knowledge, led the way with a steady determination. The spectral figure, its weakened form still lingering within the shadows, observed the group with a silent vigilance. The artifacts, held tightly by Ethan, Emma, and Lily, pulsed with an otherworldly resonance, as if sensing the impending confrontation with the dark forces that held the mansion in their thrall.

The group entered a vast chamber, its dimensions seemingly defying the architecture of the mansion. The air within the chamber was heavy with an oppressive weight, and an altar at its center bore the scars of countless forgotten rituals. Father Matthias approached the altar, his eyes scanning the symbols etched into its surface.

"These symbols are not just markings; they are keys to unlock the deeper layers of the curse," Father Matthias explained, his voice echoing within the ominous chamber. "But beware, for the forces that have bound this town in torment will not yield easily."

The family and Samuel, their eyes fixed on the altar, felt the weight of impending dread settle upon them. The townsfolk, now gathered around the chamber, exchanged uneasy glances as the shadows seemed to gather in the corners, coalescing into a palpable darkness.

Father Matthias, with an air of solemnity, began to recite incantations that echoed through the chamber. The artifacts on the altar responded, emitting a glow that danced in harmony with the priest's words. The very ground beneath their feet trembled as the symbols on the altar pulsed with an otherworldly power.

As the incantations reached a crescendo, the chamber seemed to come alive with an unseen force. The shadows contorted and writhed, forming grotesque shapes that clawed at the edges of perception. Whispers filled the air, each syllable a reminder of the ancient covenant that had bound the mansion to the forces of darkness.

Ethan, Emma, and Lily, their eyes fixed on the artifacts, saw visions of their ancestors participating in unholy rituals—dark pacts that had sealed the fate of the town for generations. Samuel, his connection to the ancient prophecy growing stronger, witnessed echoes of the choices that had set the wheels of damnation in motion.

The spectral figure, sensing the disturbance within the chamber, emerged from the shadows. Its form, though weakened, carried an aura of malevolence that seemed to defy the very laws of existence. The group, now surrounded by the swirling shadows, stood at the epicenter of a cosmic battle that transcended the boundaries of mortal understanding.

"The time has come to unveil the true nature of the curse," the spectral figure declared, its voice a haunting symphony that resonated through the chamber. "The covenant that binds this town is a pact forged in the depths of despair, and the keys to its unraveling lie within the choices made by those who dwell within its cursed walls."

Father Matthias, undeterred by the looming darkness, pressed on with the incantations. The artifacts on the altar, now bathed in a radiant glow, seemed to repel the encroaching shadows. The chamber, caught in the tug-of-war between light and darkness, quivered as if on the brink of a cataclysmic revelation.

The family and Samuel, their minds a battleground of conflicting emotions, felt the weight of ancestral sins bearing down upon them.

The townsfolk, their faces etched with a mixture of fear and anticipation, looked towards Father Matthias as a beacon of hope in the midst of the supernatural maelstrom.

As the incantations continued, the symbols on the altar began to shift and rearrange. Unearthly whispers filled the chamber, recounting the tales of forbidden bargains and sacrilegious rites that had stained the mansion's history. The air grew thick with an otherworldly energy, and the walls seemed to close in, trapping the group in a nightmarish embrace.

Ethan, Emma, and Lily, their faces pale with the weight of revelations, exchanged glances that spoke of shared horror and the burden of ancestral guilt. Samuel, caught in the currents of the ancient prophecy, felt the malevolent forces whispering promises of power and damnation. The family and Samuel, now aware of the choices that had set the curse in motion, stood at the crossroads of redemption and damnation.

The spectral figure, its form now a grotesque silhouette within the swirling shadows, spoke with a voice that carried the echoes of forgotten prophecies. "The choices made within this chamber will echo through the corridors of time. Redemption is a fragile thread, and the darkness that seeks to consume will not yield easily."

The chamber, now a battleground of cosmic forces, trembled as if caught in the throes of an otherworldly conflict. The family and Samuel, their wills tested by the malevolent forces that sought to manipulate them, stood with a collective determination that defied the encroaching darkness.

Father Matthias, with unwavering resolve, intensified the incantations. The artifacts on the altar, their glow now blinding, seemed to repel the shadows that clawed at the edges of the chamber. The townsfolk, their faces etched with awe, watched as the ancient symbols on the altar rearranged themselves, revealing a glimpse of the covenant's true nature.

"The curse is woven from the very fabric of despair, and breaking its bonds requires confronting the choices that birthed it," Father Matthias declared, his voice cutting through the supernatural maelstrom. "The symbols on this altar hold the key to unmasking the ancient forces that have ensnared this town."

As the symbols on the altar rearranged themselves, a vision unfolded before the group—a tableau of past and present, intertwined in a cosmic dance. Shadows of long-forgotten rituals played out, and the family and Samuel witnessed the choices that had damned the town to an eternity of torment.

Ethan, Emma, and Lily, their hearts heavy with the sins of their ancestors, felt the weight of a cosmic reckoning upon them. Samuel, his connection to the prophecy now fully realized, saw the threads of destiny converging upon a singular choice that could either seal the town's fate or break the shackles of damnation.

The spectral figure, its form flickering within the shadows, spoke with a voice that carried the weight of an ancient prophecy. "The symbols reveal the choices that birthed the curse. Redemption lies in unraveling the tapestry of despair and confronting the shadows that lurk within the choices made by the living and the dead."

The family and Samuel, their minds now entwined with the visions of the ancient covenant, stood on the precipice of a choice that could either damn or redeem the town. The artifacts, still pulsating with an otherworldly energy, seemed to respond to the intentions of those who held them.

Father Matthias, with a resolute gaze, addressed the group. "The symbols have shown us the path to redemption, but the choice must be made by those who bear the weight of the curse. Confront the shadows within, and break free from the chains that bind this town."

The family and Samuel, now aware of the choices that awaited them, approached the altar with a shared determination. The symbols, now frozen in a configuration that spoke of ancient bargains and tormented souls, seemed to pulse with an expectant energy.

The townsfolk, their eyes fixed on the unfolding drama, held their breath as the family and Samuel stood before the altar. The spectral figure, its form now a mere flicker within the shadows, watched with an intensity that hinted at the cosmic significance of the impending choice.

As the family and Samuel reached out to touch the symbols on the altar, a surge of energy coursed through the chamber. The shadows, as if holding their breath, seemed to recede, unveiling the raw essence of the curse that had plagued the town for centuries.

The symbols, touched by the hands of those who sought redemption, began to shift and morph. Visions of torment and ancient bargains gave way to a new configuration that spoke of sacrifice and the breaking of infernal pacts. The very air within the chamber seemed to sigh with the weight of a cosmic transformation.

"The choices made within the heart of the curse have altered the course of destiny," the spectral figure intoned, its voice carrying a sense of both resignation and hope. "The shadows may yet linger, but the chains that bound this town have been weakened by the courage to confront the darkness within."

The artifacts, now in the hands of the family and Samuel, emitted a final burst of ethereal light before settling into a dormant state. The symbols on the altar, frozen in their new configuration, seemed to resonate with the collective will of those who had dared to challenge the ancient covenant.

The chamber, once a battleground of cosmic forces, fell into an eerie stillness. The shadows, though diminished, still clung to the corners, whispering of the malevolent forces that lingered at the edges of perception. The family and Samuel, their faces etched with a mixture of exhaustion and triumph, turned towards Father Matthias with a shared understanding.

"The curse has not been fully broken, but the choices made today have set in motion a new path for this town," Father Matthias declared, his voice carrying a sense of both caution and optimism. "We must press on, confront the remaining shadows within the mansion, and uncover the final key to liberate this town from the grip of darkness."

The townsfolk, now released from the oppressive weight of the curse, looked towards the family and Samuel with a newfound hope. The spectral figure, its form now a mere whisper within the shadows, observed the group with an enigmatic gaze that hinted at the mysteries yet to be unveiled.

The family and Samuel, armed with the artifacts and the knowledge gained from the ancient symbols, prepared to face the deeper layers of the curse that still lurked within the mansion. The labyrinthine corridors, though still haunted by the echoes of the past, now seemed to hold the promise of redemption.

As the group moved deeper into the mansion, the shadows that clung to the walls seemed to retreat, as if acknowledging the shifting tides of destiny. The artifacts, though dormant, resonated with a subtle energy that guided the way forward. Father Matthias, now a beacon of hope in the midst of the supernatural darkness, led the way with a determination that echoed the collective will of those who sought to break the shackles of damnation.

The haunted mansion, its ancient secrets now partially unveiled, awaited the final confrontation with the shadows that lingered within its forsaken halls. The family and Samuel, united with the townsfolk in a shared quest for redemption, stepped into the unknown with a courage that defied the malevolent forces that sought to resist the dawning light of salvation.

Chapter 15: Echoes of Desolation - Confronting the Shadows

The group pressed on through the haunted mansion, the air heavy with an unrelenting sense of foreboding. Father Matthias led the way, his steps guided by the ancient artifacts that pulsed with a dormant energy. The family and Samuel, now attuned to the supernatural currents within the mansion, walked a tightrope between dread and determination.

As they ventured deeper, the walls of the mansion seemed to close in, bearing witness to the choices that had shaped its tortured history. The labyrinthine corridors, once a testament to forgotten secrets, now held the promise of salvation, albeit shrouded in the lingering shadows of damnation. The townsfolk, their faces etched with a mixture of hope and trepidation, followed with an unwavering trust in Father Matthias.

The group entered a chamber that seemed to defy the laws of space and time. The air within was thick with an otherworldly energy, and the walls were adorned with grotesque depictions of torment and sacrifice. At the center of the chamber stood a dais, upon which rested an ancient tome that radiated a palpable malevolence.

Father Matthias approached the dais, his eyes fixed on the ancient tome. The family and Samuel, their senses on high alert, exchanged uneasy glances as the shadows within the chamber seemed to coil with a life of their own. The artifacts, though dormant, resonated with a subtle hum, as if anticipating the revelation of the final key to break the curse.

"This tome holds the forbidden knowledge that has fueled the darkness within this mansion," Father Matthias declared, his voice carrying a weight that transcended the material world. "To unravel the remaining shadows, we must confront the tales of torment and the pact that binds this town to the forces beyond."

The family and Samuel, their eyes fixed on the ancient tome, felt the weight of the curse pressing down upon them. The townsfolk, their collective breath held in anticipation, watched as Father Matthias began to recite incantations that invoked the spirits of the past.

As the incantations reverberated through the chamber, the shadows seemed to writhe in response. Whispers echoed through the air, recounting tales of forbidden rituals and sacrilegious pacts made within the very chamber in which they stood. The walls, adorned with depictions of torment, appeared to come alive, telling a macabre story that spoke of the town's descent into darkness.

Ethan, Emma, and Lily, their minds now entwined with the ancient artifacts, saw visions of their ancestors participating in unspeakable rituals—acts of desperation that had laid the groundwork for the curse.

Samuel, his connection to the prophecy growing stronger, witnessed glimpses of the choices that had sealed the town's fate.

The spectral figure, though weakened, emerged from the shadows, its form a twisted silhouette against the macabre tapestry that adorned the chamber. The group, now surrounded by the encroaching darkness, stood at the epicenter of a supernatural confrontation that would determine the fate of the town.

"The shadows within this chamber hold the echoes of the pact that binds this town," the spectral figure intoned, its voice carrying the weight of centuries. "Confront the tales of torment, unravel the choices made within these walls, and the curse that has ensnared this town may yet be broken."

Father Matthias, undeterred by the malevolent forces that lingered within the chamber, pressed on with the incantations. The ancient tome on the dais responded, its pages fluttering as if animated by an unseen force. The artifacts in the hands of the family and Samuel, though still dormant, emitted a subtle glow that mirrored the intensity of the ritual.

As the incantations reached a crescendo, the depictions on the walls seemed to come alive. The tortured souls within the macabre illustrations writhed in agony, their silent screams echoing through the chamber. The air became charged with an otherworldly energy, and the very ground beneath their feet quivered as if in response to the cosmic forces at play.

Ethan, Emma, and Lily, their minds now fully immersed in the visions of the ancient pact, felt the weight of ancestral guilt pressing down upon them. Samuel, the bearer of the prophecy, saw the threads of destiny converging upon the choices made within the chamber. The family and Samuel, now aware of the gravity of their quest, stood with a collective resolve that defied the encroaching darkness.

The spectral figure, its form flickering within the shadows, spoke with a voice that carried the echoes of forgotten prophecies. "The tome holds the stories of despair and desperation that birthed the curse.

Confront the tales within, and the shadows that have ensnared this town may yet release their hold."

Father Matthias, with a determined gaze, opened the ancient tome. The pages, yellowed with age, revealed illustrations that depicted the choices made by the ancestors—choices that had led to the town's descent into darkness. The family and Samuel, their eyes fixed on the unfolding narrative, saw glimpses of the ancient pact that had sealed their fates.

As the illustrations unfolded, the spectral figure spoke with a sense of both sorrow and inevitability. "The curse is a consequence of choices made in times of desperation. The pact that binds this town is a tapestry woven from the threads of torment and the choices that echo through the corridors of time."

The chamber, now bathed in an otherworldly light, seemed to transcend the boundaries of reality. Visions of torment and despair played out within the illustrations, and the family and Samuel witnessed the moments that had damned the town to an eternity of suffering.

Ethan, Emma, and Lily, their hearts heavy with the sins of their ancestors, felt the weight of a cosmic reckoning upon them. Samuel, caught in the currents of the ancient prophecy, saw the choices that had set the wheels of damnation in motion.

The townsfolk, their faces etched with a mixture of horror and empathy, watched as the family and Samuel confronted the echoes of the ancient pact. The artifacts in their hands emitted a subtle glow that seemed to resonate with the revelations unfolding within the chamber.

Father Matthias, his eyes fixed on the illustrations, spoke with a voice that carried the sorrow of a town burdened by the choices of the past. "The shadows within this chamber hold the tales of torment and the choices that have cursed this town. To break the curse, we must confront the very essence of the pact that binds us."

As the group delved deeper into the stories within the ancient tome, a voice echoed through the chamber—a voice that seemed to transcend time itself. The spectral figure, its form now a mere whisper within the shadows, spoke with a resonance that carried the weight of forgotten prophecies.

"The choices made within this chamber will echo through the corridors of time. Redemption is a fragile thread, and the darkness that seeks to consume will not yield easily."

The family and Samuel, their minds now entwined with the visions of the ancient covenant, stood on the precipice of a choice that could either damn or redeem the town. The artifacts, still pulsating with an otherworldly energy, seemed to respond to the intentions of those who held them.

Father Matthias, with a resolute gaze, addressed the group. "The symbols have shown us the path to redemption, but the choice must be made by those who bear the weight of the curse. Confront the shadows within, and break free from the chains that bind this town."

The family and Samuel, now aware of the choices that awaited them, approached the altar with a shared determination. The symbols, now frozen in a configuration that spoke of ancient bargains and tormented souls, seemed to pulse with an expectant energy.

The townsfolk, their eyes fixed on the unfolding drama, held their breath as the family and Samuel stood before the altar. The spectral figure, its form now a mere flicker within the shadows, watched with an intensity that hinted at the mysteries yet to be unveiled.

As the family and Samuel reached out to touch the symbols on the altar, a surge of energy coursed through the chamber. The shadows, as if holding their breath, seemed to recede, unveiling the raw essence of the curse that had plagued the town for centuries.

The symbols, touched by the hands of those who sought redemption, began to shift and morph. Visions of torment and ancient bargains gave way to a new configuration that spoke of sacrifice and the breaking of infernal pacts. The very air within the chamber seemed to sigh with the weight of a cosmic transformation.

"The choices made within the heart of the curse have altered the course of destiny," the spectral figure intoned, its voice carrying a sense of both resignation and hope. "The shadows may yet linger, but the chains that bound this town have been weakened by the courage to confront the darkness within."

The artifacts, now in the hands of the family and Samuel, emitted a final burst of ethereal light before settling into a dormant state. The symbols on the altar, frozen in their new configuration, seemed to resonate with the collective will of those who had dared to challenge the ancient covenant.

The chamber, once a battleground of cosmic forces, fell into an eerie stillness. The shadows, though diminished, still clung to the corners, whispering of the malevolent forces that lingered at the edges of perception. The family and Samuel, their faces etched with a mixture of exhaustion and triumph, turned towards Father Matthias with a shared understanding.

"The curse has not been fully broken, but the choices made today have set in motion a new path for this town," Father Matthias declared, his voice carrying a sense of both caution and optimism. "We must press on, confront the remaining shadows within the mansion, and uncover the final key to liberate this town from the grip of darkness."

The townsfolk, now released from the oppressive weight of the curse, looked towards the family and Samuel with a newfound hope. The spectral figure, its form now a mere whisper within the shadows, observed the group with an enigmatic gaze that hinted at the mysteries yet to be unveiled.

The family and Samuel, armed with the artifacts and the knowledge gained from the ancient symbols, prepared to face the deeper layers of the curse that still lurked within the mansion. The labyrinthine corridors, though still haunted by the echoes of the past, now seemed to hold the promise of redemption.

As the group moved deeper into the mansion, the shadows that clung to the walls seemed to retreat, as if acknowledging the shifting tides of destiny. The artifacts, though dormant, resonated with a subtle energy that guided the way forward. Father Matthias, now a beacon of hope in the midst of the supernatural darkness, led the way with a determination that echoed the collective will of those who sought to break the shackles of damnation.

The haunted mansion, its ancient secrets now partially unveiled, awaited the final confrontation with the shadows that lingered within its forsaken halls. The family and Samuel, united with the townsfolk in a shared quest for redemption, stepped into the unknown with a courage that defied the malevolent forces that sought to resist the dawning light of salvation.

Chapter 16: The Abyss Beckons - Unveiling the Final Key

The group, guided by the subtle energy resonating from the artifacts, pressed deeper into the mansion. Father Matthias led with an unwavering determination, the weight of the ancient artifacts in the hands of Ethan, Emma, and Lily serving as both a guide and a reminder of the cosmic forces at play. Samuel, his connection to the prophecy now a steady pulse within him, walked with a sense of purpose that transcended mortal understanding.

The corridors seemed to warp and twist, as if the very fabric of reality protested their intrusion into the deeper layers of the mansion's secrets. Shadows clung to the walls like sentient entities, whispering of the malevolent forces that awaited their arrival. The family and Samuel, their senses heightened by the artifacts, walked on the precipice of a nightmare, their breaths synchronized in the face of the unknown.

They entered a chamber unlike any before—a vast expanse that defied the mansion's architectural logic. The air within was charged with an eerie energy, and the artifacts pulsed with a subtle glow, resonating with the dormant power hidden within the mansion's depths. At the center of the chamber stood an ancient altar, upon which rested a relic of unimaginable darkness—a dagger forged from the very shadows that clung to the walls.

Father Matthias, his eyes fixed on the malevolent relic, spoke with a solemnity that cut through the tension in the chamber. "This dagger, forged from the shadows themselves, is the final key to unraveling the curse that has ensnared this town. But beware, for its power is both a means of salvation and a conduit to the darkest abyss."

The family and Samuel, their gaze drawn to the ominous dagger, felt the weight of the ancient artifact pressing down upon them. The townsfolk, gathered at the chamber entrance, exchanged wary glances, their trust in Father Matthias now tinged with the realization that the road to redemption would be paved with unimaginable challenges.

As Father Matthias approached the altar, the shadows within the chamber seemed to congregate, coalescing around the dagger as if acknowledging its malevolent power. The artifacts in the hands of the family emitted a subtle hum, resonating with a frequency that hinted at the cosmic forces about to be unleashed.

"The dagger is a manifestation of the darkness that birthed the curse," Father Matthias intoned, his voice echoing through the chamber. "To break the shackles that bind this town, we must confront the very essence of the shadows that linger within this artifact."

The family and Samuel, their hearts now synchronized with the artifacts, watched as Father Matthias began to recite incantations that invoked the ancient powers hidden within the dagger. The shadows, responsive to the incantations, danced around the altar in a macabre display of supernatural energy.

Ethan, Emma, and Lily, their minds now entwined with the artifacts, saw visions of the dagger's creation—a ritual that harnessed the very essence of the abyss. Samuel, the bearer of the prophecy, felt the currents of ancient power coursing through the chamber, whispering promises of both damnation and salvation.

The spectral figure, though weakened, emerged from the shadows, its form a grotesque silhouette against the cosmic tapestry unfolding within the chamber. The group, now surrounded by the encroaching darkness, stood at the epicenter of a supernatural convergence that would determine the town's ultimate fate.

"The dagger is a conduit to the abyss, a gateway to the forces that defy mortal comprehension," the spectral figure declared, its voice carrying the echoes of forgotten prophecies. "To wield its power is to dance on the edge of damnation, and the choices made within this chamber will resonate through the corridors of time."

Father Matthias, undeterred by the malevolent forces that sought to resist the dagger's awakening, pressed on with the incantations. The ancient relic on the altar responded, its shadowy form pulsating with an otherworldly glow. The artifacts in the hands of the family, though dormant, emitted a subtle energy that seemed to harmonize with the ritual unfolding before them.

As the incantations reached a crescendo, the dagger's glow intensified. The shadows within the chamber seemed to converge, forming a swirling vortex of darkness that encircled the ancient artifact. The air became charged with an otherworldly energy, and the very ground beneath their feet trembled as if in anticipation of the cosmic forces at play.

Ethan, Emma, and Lily, their minds now fully immersed in the visions of the dagger's creation, felt the weight of ancestral sins pressing down upon them. Samuel, the conduit to the prophecy, saw the threads of destiny converging upon the choices made within the chamber. The family and Samuel, now aware of the gravity of their quest, stood with a collective resolve that defied the encroaching darkness.

The spectral figure, its form flickering within the shadows, spoke with a voice that carried the echoes of forgotten prophecies. "The dagger holds the essence of the abyss, a power that can either damn or redeem. Confront the shadows within its core, and the choices made within this chamber will shape the destiny of this town."

Father Matthias, with unwavering resolve, extended his hands towards the dagger. The artifacts in the hands of the family emitted a subtle glow that seemed to respond to the ancient relic's awakening. The townsfolk, their faces etched with a mixture of awe and trepidation, watched as the cosmic forces within the chamber reached a fevered pitch.

"The abyss beckons, and the choices made within its embrace will echo through the annals of time," Father Matthias declared, his voice cutting through the supernatural maelstrom. "We stand at the threshold of redemption and damnation, and the path we choose within this chamber will determine the fate of this town."

As the dagger's glow intensified, the spectral figure spoke with a sense of both caution and inevitability. "The shadows within the dagger are a reflection of the choices made by those who sought power and salvation. Confront the darkness, and the path to redemption may yet be revealed."

The family and Samuel, their minds now entwined with the artifacts and the ancient relic, approached the altar with a shared determination. The dagger, its shadowy form pulsating with an otherworldly energy, seemed to respond to the intentions of those who stood before it.

The townsfolk, their eyes fixed on the unfolding drama, held their breath as the family and Samuel stood before the altar. The spectral figure, its form now a mere flicker within the shadows, watched with an intensity that hinted at the mysteries yet to be unveiled.

As the family and Samuel reached out to touch the dagger, a surge of energy coursed through the chamber. The shadows, as if alive, recoiled before converging around the ancient relic. The very air within the chamber seemed to vibrate with the cosmic forces unleashed by the group's touch.

The dagger, touched by the hands of those who sought redemption, began to shift and morph. Visions of torment and the abyss gave way to a new configuration that spoke of sacrifice and the breaking of infernal pacts. The very fabric of the chamber seemed to shudder as the cosmic transformation took hold.

"The choices made within the heart of the abyss have altered the course of destiny," the spectral figure intoned, its voice carrying a sense of both resignation and hope. "The shadows may yet linger, but the chains that bound this town have been weakened by the courage to confront the darkness within."

The artifacts, now in the hands of the family and Samuel, emitted a final burst of ethereal light before settling into a dormant state. The dagger, its malevolent glow subdued, seemed to resonate with the collective will of those who had dared to challenge the ancient covenant.

The chamber, once a battleground of cosmic forces, fell into an eerie stillness. The shadows, though diminished, still clung to the corners, whispering of the malevolent forces that lingered at the edges of perception. The family and Samuel, their faces etched with a mixture of exhaustion and triumph, turned towards Father Matthias with a shared understanding.

"The curse has not been fully broken, but the choices made today have set in motion a new path for this town," Father Matthias declared, his voice carrying a sense of both caution and optimism. "We must press on, confront the remaining shadows within the mansion, and uncover the final key to liberate this town from the grip of darkness."

The townsfolk, now released from the oppressive weight of the curse, looked towards the family and Samuel with a newfound hope. The spectral figure, its form now a mere whisper within the shadows, observed the group with an enigmatic gaze that hinted at the mysteries yet to be unveiled.

The family and Samuel, armed with the artifacts, the knowledge gained from the ancient symbols, and the essence of the abyss contained within the dagger, prepared to face the deeper layers of the curse that still lurked within the mansion. The labyrinthine corridors, though still haunted by the echoes of the past, now seemed to hold the promise of redemption.

As the group moved deeper into the mansion, the shadows that clung to the walls seemed to retreat, as if acknowledging the shifting tides of destiny. The artifacts, though dormant, resonated with a subtle energy that guided the way forward. Father Matthias, now a beacon of hope in the midst of the supernatural darkness, led the way with a determination that echoed the collective will of those who sought to break the shackles of damnation.

The haunted mansion, its ancient secrets now partially unveiled, awaited the final confrontation with the shadows that lingered within its forsaken halls. The family and Samuel, united with the townsfolk in a shared quest for redemption, stepped into the unknown with a courage that defied the malevolent forces that sought to resist the dawning light of salvation.

Chapter 17: The Labyrinth of Torment - Unearthing the Hidden Malevolence

The group advanced through the mansion's depths, the artifacts now pulsating with an ethereal glow that cast a feeble light on the foreboding corridors. Father Matthias, his resolve unbroken despite the challenges faced, led the way with a torch in hand, the flames flickering as if resisting the supernatural forces that sought to snuff them out.

The labyrinthine halls seemed to twist and turn with a malevolent intent, as if reshaping themselves to confound the intruders. Shadows clung to the walls like sentient entities, whispering of ancient grievances and foretelling the impending confrontation. The family and Samuel, their senses attuned to the artifacts, moved forward with a shared determination that bordered on defiance.

They entered a chamber that defied the laws of physics—an unsettling blend of reality and nightmare. The air within was thick with an oppressive energy, and the artifacts emitted a subtle hum that resonated with the malevolence hidden within the mansion's recesses. At the center of the chamber stood a cursed relic—a mirror that reflected not only the physical form but also the deepest fears and regrets of those who gazed into its surface.

Father Matthias, his eyes fixed on the malevolent mirror, spoke with a somber tone that betrayed the gravity of the challenge ahead. "This mirror holds the echoes of torment and regret, a gateway to the darkest recesses of the soul. To confront the hidden malevolence within is to face the true nature of the curse that plagues this town."

The family and Samuel, their gaze drawn to the ominous mirror, felt a chill in the air as if the very fabric of reality recoiled from the malevolent forces contained within the cursed relic. The townsfolk, lingering at the chamber entrance, exchanged uneasy glances, their trust in Father Matthias now tinged with the realization that the road to redemption led through the shadows of damnation.

As Father Matthias approached the mirror, the artifacts in the hands of the family emitted a subtle glow, as if resonating with the dormant power concealed within the cursed relic. The mirror, reflecting the chamber's distorted reality, seemed to ripple with a supernatural energy that mirrored the cosmic forces at play.

"The mirror is a vessel of hidden malevolence, a reflection of the choices that birthed the curse," Father Matthias intoned, his voice echoing through the chamber. "To break the shackles that bind this town, we must confront the shadows that lurk within the souls reflected in this cursed glass."

The family and Samuel, their hearts now synchronized with the artifacts, watched as Father Matthias began to recite incantations that invoked the ancient powers hidden within the mirror. The shadows, responsive to the incantations, seemed to writhe within the glass, whispering secrets of despair and regret.

Ethan, Emma, and Lily, their minds now entwined with the artifacts, saw visions of their own fears and regrets reflected in the cursed mirror—haunting images that spoke of choices made and consequences borne. Samuel, the bearer of the prophecy, felt the currents of ancient power coursing through the chamber, whispering promises of both damnation and redemption.

The spectral figure, though weakened, emerged from the shadows, its form a grotesque silhouette against the kaleidoscopic display within the mirror. The group, now surrounded by the encroaching darkness, stood at the epicenter of a supernatural convergence that would determine the town's ultimate fate.

"The mirror reflects the hidden malevolence within, a truth that cannot be concealed," the spectral figure declared, its voice carrying the echoes of forgotten prophecies. "To confront the shadows within the souls reflected is to unveil the essence of the curse that binds this town."

Father Matthias, undeterred by the malevolent forces that sought to resist the mirror's awakening, pressed on with the incantations. The cursed relic responded, its surface rippling with the reflections of tormented souls. The artifacts in the hands of the family, though dormant, emitted a subtle energy that seemed to harmonize with the ritual unfolding before them.

As the incantations reached a crescendo, the reflections within the mirror seemed to come alive. The tortured souls trapped within its surface writhed in agony, their silent screams echoing through the chamber. The air became charged with an otherworldly energy, and the very ground beneath their feet quivered as if in anticipation of the cosmic forces at play.

Ethan, Emma, and Lily, their minds now fully immersed in the visions of the mirror, felt the weight of their hidden fears pressing down upon them. Samuel, the conduit to the prophecy, saw the threads of destiny converging upon the choices reflected in the cursed glass. The family and Samuel, now aware of the gravity of their quest, stood with a collective resolve that defied the encroaching darkness.

The spectral figure, its form flickering within the shadows, spoke with a voice that carried the echoes of forgotten prophecies. "The mirror holds the reflections of torment and regret, a testament to the choices that have bound this town. Confront the darkness within the souls reflected, and the path to redemption may yet be revealed."

Father Matthias, with unwavering resolve, extended his hands towards the mirror. The artifacts in the hands of the family emitted a subtle glow that seemed to respond to the ancient relic's awakening. The townsfolk, their faces etched with a mixture of awe and trepidation, watched as the cosmic forces within the chamber reached a fevered pitch.

"The mirror reflects the hidden truths that lie dormant within the soul," Father Matthias declared, his voice cutting through the supernatural maelstrom. "We stand at the threshold of revelation, and the choices we make within the gaze of this cursed glass will determine the fate of this town."

As the mirror's reflections intensified, the spectral figure spoke with a sense of both caution and inevitability. "The shadows within the mirror are a reflection of the choices made by those who sought to hide their true selves. Confront the darkness, and the path to redemption may yet be revealed."

The family and Samuel, their minds now entwined with the artifacts and the cursed relic, approached the mirror with a shared determination. The reflections within the cursed glass, distorted and tormented, seemed to respond to the intentions of those who stood before it.

The townsfolk, their eyes fixed on the unfolding drama, held their breath as the family and Samuel stood before the mirror. The spectral figure, its form now a mere flicker within the shadows, watched with an intensity that hinted at the mysteries yet to be unveiled.

As the family and Samuel reached out to touch the mirror, a surge of energy coursed through the chamber. The shadows within the mirror, as if alive, recoiled before reshaping into new reflections. The very air within the chamber seemed to vibrate with the cosmic forces unleashed by the group's touch.

The reflections within the mirror, touched by the hands of those who sought redemption, began to shift and morph. Visions of torment and hidden regrets gave way to a new configuration that spoke of self-discovery and the breaking of internal chains. The very fabric of the chamber seemed to sigh with the weight of a cosmic transformation.

"The choices made within the gaze of the mirror have altered the course of destiny," the spectral figure intoned, its voice carrying a sense of both resignation and hope. "The shadows may yet linger, but the chains that bound this town have been weakened by the courage to confront the darkness within."

The artifacts, now in the hands of the family and Samuel, emitted a final burst of ethereal light before settling into a dormant state. The mirror, its malevolent reflections now subdued, seemed to resonate with the collective will of those who had dared to challenge the hidden malevolence.

The chamber, once a battleground of cosmic forces, fell into an eerie stillness. The shadows, though diminished, still clung to the corners, whispering of the malevolent forces that lingered at the edges of perception. The family and Samuel, their faces etched with a mixture of exhaustion and triumph, turned towards Father Matthias with a shared understanding.

"The curse has not been fully broken, but the choices made today have set in motion a new path for this town," Father Matthias declared, his voice carrying a sense of both caution and optimism. "We must press on, confront the remaining shadows within the mansion, and uncover the final key to liberate this town from the grip of darkness."

The townsfolk, now released from the oppressive weight of the curse, looked towards the family and Samuel with a newfound hope. The spectral figure, its form now a mere whisper within the shadows, observed the group with an enigmatic gaze that hinted at the mysteries yet to be unveiled.

The family and Samuel, armed with the artifacts, the knowledge gained from the ancient symbols, the essence of the abyss contained within the dagger, and the revelations extracted from the mirror, prepared to face the deeper layers of the curse that still lurked within the mansion. The labyrinthine corridors, though still haunted by the echoes of the past, now seemed to hold the promise of redemption.

As the group moved deeper into the mansion, the shadows that clung to the walls seemed to retreat, as if acknowledging the shifting tides of destiny. The artifacts, though dormant, resonated with a subtle energy that guided the way forward. Father Matthias, now a beacon of hope in the midst of the supernatural darkness, led the way with a determination that echoed the collective will of those who sought to break the shackles of damnation.

The haunted mansion, its ancient secrets now partially unveiled, awaited the final confrontation with the shadows that lingered within its forsaken halls. The family and Samuel, united with the townsfolk in a shared quest for redemption, stepped into the unknown with a courage that defied the malevolent forces that sought to resist the dawning light of salvation.

Chapter 18: The Abyss Unleashed - Confronting the Malevolent Entity

The group ventured deeper into the mansion, the artifacts in hand now resonating with an unsettling energy. The labyrinthine corridors seemed to warp and twist, the very walls pulsating with a malevolence that mocked the intruders. Father Matthias, his torch flickering in the oppressive darkness, led the way with a determination that defied the supernatural forces resisting their advance.

As they approached a grand chamber adorned with ancient symbols and foreboding statuary, a palpable tension hung in the air. Shadows clung to the walls like sentient tendrils, their whispers weaving a tapestry of dread. The artifacts in the family's hands emitted an ominous hum, responding to the latent power concealed within the mansion's depths.

At the center of the chamber stood an altar bathed in an ethereal glow. Upon it lay a tattered tome, bound in human skin and adorned with infernal symbols. Father Matthias, recognizing the ancient grimoire, spoke with a voice that carried the weight of forbidden knowledge. "This tome is the key to unmasking the malevolent entity that festers within the heart of the curse. Its pages reveal the darkest secrets and the incantations that can either bind or unleash the abyss."

The family and Samuel, their eyes fixed on the forbidden tome, felt a shiver run down their spines. The townsfolk, lingering at the chamber entrance, exchanged uneasy glances, their trust in Father Matthias now intertwined with a growing sense of trepidation.

As Father Matthias approached the altar, the artifacts in the family's hands emitted an eerie glow, resonating with the dormant power concealed within the ancient grimoire. The malevolent entity, sensing the intrusion, sent ripples through the shadows, as if testing the resolve of those who dared to challenge its dominion.

"The tome is a repository of forbidden knowledge, a compendium of the abyss's darkest secrets," Father Matthias intoned, his voice cutting through the uneasy silence. "To confront the malevolent entity, we must delve into the infernal incantations and expose the very essence of the curse that plagues this town."

The family and Samuel, their hearts now synchronized with the artifacts, watched as Father Matthias opened the tome. The pages, filled with archaic symbols and demonic incantations, seemed to come alive with an unholy energy. The malevolent entity, aware of the imminent confrontation, sent ripples through the shadows, as if mocking the futile efforts to resist its influence.

Ethan, Emma, and Lily, their minds now entwined with the artifacts, saw visions of the malevolent entity's awakening—an ancient force that thrived on despair and sought to consume the very souls of the living. Samuel, the bearer of the prophecy, felt the currents of ancient power coursing through the chamber, whispering promises of both damnation and salvation.

The spectral figure, though weakened, emerged from the shadows, its form a grotesque silhouette against the spectral glow emanating from the tome. The group, now surrounded by the encroaching darkness, stood at the epicenter of a supernatural convergence that would determine the town's ultimate fate.

"The tome holds the incantations that bind the malevolent entity to the curse," the spectral figure declared, its voice carrying the echoes of forgotten prophecies. "To confront the shadows within its pages is to challenge the very essence of the abyss that festers within this mansion."

Father Matthias, undeterred by the malevolent forces that sought to resist the tome's opening, pressed on with the incantations. The ancient grimoire responded, its pages turning as if guided by an unseen hand. The artifacts in the family's hands, though dormant, emitted a subtle energy that seemed to harmonize with the ritual unfolding before them.

As the incantations reached a crescendo, the chamber seemed to come alive with an otherworldly energy. Shadows, infused with the malevolent entity's influence, writhed around the altar, forming a grotesque dance of darkness. The air became charged with an oppressive force, and the very ground beneath their feet trembled as if in anticipation of the cosmic forces at play.

Ethan, Emma, and Lily, their minds now fully immersed in the visions of the tome, felt the weight of ancient malevolence pressing down upon them. Samuel, the conduit to the prophecy, saw the threads of destiny converging upon the choices made within the chamber. The family and Samuel, now aware of the gravity of their quest, stood with a collective resolve that defied the encroaching darkness.

The spectral figure, its form flickering within the shadows, spoke with a voice that carried the echoes of forgotten prophecies. "The tome holds the incantations that have bound this town to the abyss. Confront the shadows within its pages, and the choices made within this chamber will resonate through the corridors of time."

Father Matthias, with unwavering resolve, extended his hands towards the tome. The artifacts in the family's hands emitted a subtle glow that seemed to respond to the ancient grimoire's awakening. The townsfolk, their faces etched with a mixture of awe and trepidation, watched as the cosmic forces within the chamber reached a fevered pitch.

"The abyss beckons, and the choices made within its pages will echo through the annals of time," Father Matthias declared, his voice cutting through the supernatural maelstrom. "We stand at the precipice of revelation, and the choices we make within this chamber will determine the fate of this town."

As the tome's spectral glow intensified, the spectral figure spoke with a sense of both caution and inevitability. "The shadows within the pages are a reflection of the choices made by those who sought power and salvation. Confront the darkness, and the path to redemption may yet be revealed."

The family and Samuel, their minds now entwined with the artifacts and the ancient grimoire, approached the altar with a shared determination. The pages of the tome, infused with the malevolent entity's influence, seemed to respond to the intentions of those who stood before it.

The townsfolk, their eyes fixed on the unfolding drama, held their breath as the family and Samuel stood before the altar. The spectral figure, its form now a mere flicker within the shadows, watched with an intensity that hinted at the mysteries yet to be unveiled.

As the family and Samuel reached out to touch the tome, a surge of energy coursed through the chamber. The shadows within the pages, as if alive, recoiled before reshaping into new incantations. The very air within the chamber seemed to vibrate with the cosmic forces unleashed by the group's touch.

The pages of the tome, touched by the hands of those who sought redemption, began to shift and morph. Visions of torment and infernal pacts gave way to a new configuration that spoke of sacrifice and the breaking of ancient curses. The very fabric of the chamber seemed to sigh with the weight of a cosmic transformation.

"The choices made within the heart of the abyss have altered the course of destiny," the spectral figure intoned, its voice carrying a sense of both resignation and hope. "The shadows may yet linger, but the chains that bound this town have been weakened by the courage to confront the darkness within."

The artifacts, now in the hands of the family and Samuel, emitted a final burst of ethereal light before settling into a dormant state. The tome, its spectral glow subdued, seemed to resonate with the collective will of those who had dared to challenge the malevolent entity.

The chamber, once a battleground of cosmic forces, fell into an eerie stillness. The shadows, though diminished, still clung to the corners, whispering of the malevolent forces that lingered at the edges of perception. The family and Samuel, their faces etched with a mixture of exhaustion and triumph, turned towards Father Matthias with a shared understanding.

"The curse has not been fully broken, but the choices made today have set in motion a new path for this town," Father Matthias declared, his voice carrying a sense of both caution and optimism. "We must press on, confront the remaining shadows within the mansion, and uncover the final key to liberate this town from the grip of darkness."

The townsfolk, now released from the oppressive weight of the curse, looked towards the family and Samuel with a newfound hope. The spectral figure, its form now a mere whisper within the shadows, observed the group with an enigmatic gaze that hinted at the mysteries yet to be unveiled.

The family and Samuel, armed with the artifacts, the knowledge gained from the ancient symbols, the essence of the abyss contained within the dagger, the revelations extracted from the mirror, and the incantations deciphered from the tome, prepared to face the deeper layers of the curse that still lurked within the mansion. The labyrinthine corridors, though still haunted by the echoes of the past, now seemed to hold the promise of redemption.

As the group moved deeper into the mansion, the shadows that clung to the walls seemed to retreat, as if acknowledging the shifting tides of destiny. The artifacts, though dormant, resonated with a subtle energy that guided the way forward. Father Matthias, now a beacon of hope in the midst of the supernatural darkness, led the way with a determination that echoed the collective will of those who sought to break the shackles of damnation.

The haunted mansion, its ancient secrets now partially unveiled, awaited the final confrontation with the shadows that lingered within its forsaken halls. The family and Samuel, united with the townsfolk in a shared quest for redemption, stepped into the unknown with a courage that defied the malevolent forces that sought to resist the dawning light of salvation.

Chapter 19: The Veil of Despair - Gateway to the Abyss

The group pressed on, the corridors twisting and turning with an eerie determination to confound their advance. Father Matthias, the artifacts in hand, led the way through the oppressive darkness, the torch's feeble light flickering against the encroaching shadows. A sense of foreboding hung in the air, as if the mansion itself recoiled from the impending confrontation.

As they entered a chamber cloaked in an unnatural gloom, the artifacts in the family's hands emitted a subtle glow, resonating with the latent power concealed within the mansion's depths. The air seemed to thicken with a malevolence that whispered of the horrors yet to be unveiled. At the center of the chamber stood an ancient doorway, adorned with symbols that seemed to writhe with a life of their own.

Father Matthias, his eyes fixed on the malevolent gateway, spoke with a gravity that mirrored the weight of the curse. "This doorway is the final threshold, the veil that separates our world from the abyss. To confront the malevolent forces that lurk beyond is to challenge the very heart of the curse that has ensnared this town."

The family and Samuel, their gaze drawn to the ominous gateway, felt a chill in the air as if the very fabric of reality trembled at the prospect of what lay beyond. The townsfolk, lingering at the chamber entrance, exchanged wary glances, their trust in Father Matthias now intertwined with the growing uncertainty of what awaited them.

As Father Matthias approached the doorway, the artifacts in the family's hands emitted an eerie glow, responding to the dormant power concealed within the ancient gateway. The malevolent forces, sensing the intrusion, sent ripples through the shadows, as if mocking the futile efforts to resist their dominion.

"The doorway is a passage to the abyss, a gateway to the malevolent forces that thrive on despair," Father Matthias intoned, his voice echoing through the chamber. "To break the shackles that bind this town, we must confront the shadows that linger beyond this cursed threshold."

The family and Samuel, their hearts now synchronized with the artifacts, watched as Father Matthias began to recite incantations that invoked the ancient powers hidden within the doorway. The symbols on the gateway seemed to writhe and twist, reacting to the supernatural forces at play.

Ethan, Emma, and Lily, their minds now entwined with the artifacts, saw visions of the abyss beyond the gateway—an expanse of darkness teeming with malevolent entities and echoing with the tormented cries of lost souls. Samuel, the bearer of the prophecy, felt the currents of ancient power coursing through the chamber, whispering promises of both damnation and salvation.

The spectral figure, though weakened, emerged from the shadows, its form a grotesque silhouette against the spectral glow emanating from the gateway. The group, now surrounded by the encroaching darkness, stood at the epicenter of a supernatural convergence that would determine the town's ultimate fate.

"The gateway is the veil that separates our world from the abyss, a passage forged by the choices that birthed the curse," the spectral figure declared, its voice carrying the echoes of forgotten prophecies. "To confront the shadows beyond is to unveil the essence of the curse that plagues this town."

Father Matthias, undeterred by the malevolent forces that sought to resist the gateway's opening, pressed on with the incantations. The ancient symbols responded, shifting and pulsating as if aligning with the cosmic forces at play. The artifacts in the family's hands, though dormant, emitted a subtle energy that seemed to harmonize with the ritual unfolding before them.

As the incantations reached a crescendo, the gateway seemed to ripple with an otherworldly energy. Shadows, infused with the malevolent forces' influence, danced around the doorway, forming a grotesque display of supernatural power. The air became charged with an oppressive force, and the very ground beneath their feet quivered as if in anticipation of the cosmic forces at play.

Ethan, Emma, and Lily, their minds now fully immersed in the visions of the abyss, felt the weight of ancient malevolence pressing down upon them. Samuel, the conduit to the prophecy, saw the threads of destiny converging upon the choices made within the chamber. The family and Samuel, now aware of the gravity of their quest, stood with a collective resolve that defied the encroaching darkness.

The spectral figure, its form flickering within the shadows, spoke with a voice that carried the echoes of forgotten prophecies. "The gateway is the passage to the abyss, a reflection of the choices made by those who sought power and salvation. Confront the darkness beyond, and the choices made within this chamber will resonate through the corridors of time."

Father Matthias, with unwavering resolve, extended his hands towards the gateway. The artifacts in the family's hands emitted a subtle glow that seemed to respond to the ancient gateway's awakening. The townsfolk, their faces etched with a mixture of awe and trepidation, watched as the cosmic forces within the chamber reached a fevered pitch.

"The abyss beckons, and the choices made within its embrace will echo through the annals of time," Father Matthias declared, his voice cutting through the supernatural maelstrom. "We stand at the precipice of revelation, and the choices we make within this chamber will determine the fate of this town."

As the gateway's spectral glow intensified, the spectral figure spoke with a sense of both caution and inevitability. "The shadows beyond the gateway are a reflection of the choices made by those who sought power and salvation. Confront the darkness, and the path to redemption may yet be revealed."

The family and Samuel, their minds now entwined with the artifacts and the gateway, approached the ominous threshold with a shared determination. The symbols on the gateway, infused with the malevolent forces' influence, seemed to respond to the intentions of those who stood before it.

The townsfolk, their eyes fixed on the unfolding drama, held their breath as the family and Samuel stood before the gateway. The spectral figure, its form now a mere flicker within the shadows, watched with an intensity that hinted at the mysteries yet to be unveiled.

As the family and Samuel reached out to touch the gateway, a surge of energy coursed through the chamber. The shadows around the doorway, as if alive, recoiled before reshaping into new configurations. The very air within the chamber seemed to vibrate with the cosmic forces unleashed by the group's touch.

The gateway, touched by the hands of those who sought redemption, began to shift and morph. Visions of the abyss and the malevolent entities gave way to a new configuration that spoke of sacrifice and the breaking of ancient curses. The very fabric of the chamber seemed to sigh with the weight of a cosmic transformation.

"The choices made within the heart of the abyss have altered the course of destiny," the spectral figure intoned, its voice carrying a sense of both resignation and hope. "The shadows may yet linger, but the chains that bound this town have been weakened by the courage to confront the darkness within."

The artifacts, now in the hands of the family and Samuel, emitted a final burst of ethereal light before settling into a dormant state. The gateway, its spectral glow subdued, seemed to resonate with the collective will of those who had dared to challenge the abyss.

The chamber, once a battleground of cosmic forces, fell into an eerie stillness. The shadows, though diminished, still clung to the corners, whispering of the malevolent forces that lingered at the edges of perception. The family and Samuel, their faces etched with a mixture of exhaustion and triumph, turned towards Father Matthias with a shared understanding.

"The curse has not been fully broken, but the choices made today have set in motion a new path for this town," Father Matthias declared, his voice carrying a sense of both caution and optimism. "We must press on, confront the remaining shadows within the mansion, and uncover the final key to liberate this town from the grip of darkness."

The townsfolk, now released from the oppressive weight of the curse, looked towards the family and Samuel with a newfound hope. The spectral figure, its form now a mere whisper within the shadows, observed the group with an enigmatic gaze that hinted at the mysteries yet to be unveiled.

The family and Samuel, armed with the artifacts, the knowledge gained from the ancient symbols, the essence of the abyss contained within the dagger, the revelations extracted from the mirror, the incantations deciphered from the tome, and the courage to challenge the malevolent forces beyond the gateway, prepared to face the final layers of the curse that still lurked within the mansion. The labyrinthine corridors, though still haunted by the echoes of the past, now seemed to hold the promise of redemption.

As the group moved deeper into the mansion, the shadows that clung to the walls seemed to retreat, as if acknowledging the shifting tides of destiny. The artifacts, though dormant, resonated with a subtle energy that guided the way forward. Father Matthias, now a beacon of hope in the midst of the supernatural darkness, led the way with a determination that echoed the collective will of those who sought to break the shackles of damnation.

The haunted mansion, its ancient secrets now partially unveiled, awaited the final confrontation with the shadows that lingered within its forsaken halls. The family and Samuel, united with the townsfolk in a shared quest for redemption, stepped into the unknown with a courage that defied the malevolent forces that sought to resist the dawning light of salvation.

Chapter 20: The Abyssal Reckoning - Unveiling the Final Confrontation

The group ventured deeper into the mansion, the air growing heavier with an oppressive anticipation. The artifacts in the family's hands emitted an unsettling energy, as if resonating with the very heartbeat of the malevolent forces that lingered within the forsaken halls. Father Matthias, undeterred by the shadows that clung to the walls, led the way with the torch held high, its feeble light flickering against the encroaching darkness.

As they entered a cavernous chamber, the artifacts in the family's hands pulsed with an otherworldly glow. The symbols etched into the walls seemed to come alive, casting grotesque shadows that danced in a macabre display. At the center of the chamber stood an ancient altar, adorned with eerie carvings and bathed in an unholy radiance.

Father Matthias, his eyes fixed on the malevolent altar, spoke with a solemnity that betrayed the gravity of the moment. "This altar is the epicenter of the curse, the convergence point of the malevolent forces that seek to consume this town. To confront the abyss that festers within is to challenge the very heart of darkness."

The family and Samuel, their gaze drawn to the sinister altar, felt a chill in the air as if the very fabric of reality quivered at the impending confrontation. The townsfolk, lingering at the chamber entrance, exchanged uneasy glances, their trust in Father Matthias now intertwined with a growing sense of dread.

As Father Matthias approached the altar, the artifacts in the family's hands emitted an eerie glow, resonating with the dormant power concealed within the malevolent structure. The malevolent forces, sensing the intrusion, sent ripples through the shadows, as if mocking the futile efforts to resist their dominion.

"The altar is the focal point of the abyss, a conduit through which the malevolent forces draw power," Father Matthias intoned, his voice echoing through the chamber. "To break the shackles that bind this town, we must confront the malevolent forces that linger at the very heart of this cursed mansion."

The family and Samuel, their hearts now synchronized with the artifacts, watched as Father Matthias began to recite incantations that invoked the ancient powers hidden within the altar. The symbols on the walls seemed to writhe and twist, reacting to the supernatural forces at play.

Ethan, Emma, and Lily, their minds now entwined with the artifacts, saw visions of the abyss that emanated from the altar—an expanse of darkness teeming with malevolent entities and echoing with the tormented cries of lost souls. Samuel, the bearer of the prophecy, felt the currents of ancient power coursing through the chamber, whispering promises of both damnation and salvation.

The spectral figure, though weakened, emerged from the shadows, its form a grotesque silhouette against the unholy radiance emanating from the altar. The group, now surrounded by the encroaching darkness, stood at the epicenter of a supernatural convergence that would determine the town's ultimate fate.

"The altar is the conduit through which the malevolent forces draw sustenance," the spectral figure declared, its voice carrying the echoes of forgotten prophecies. "To confront the shadows within its unholy radiance is to unveil the essence of the abyss that plagues this town."

Father Matthias, undeterred by the malevolent forces that sought to resist the altar's awakening, pressed on with the incantations. The symbols on the walls responded, shifting and pulsating as if aligning with the cosmic forces at play. The artifacts in the family's hands, though dormant, emitted a subtle energy that seemed to harmonize with the ritual unfolding before them.

As the incantations reached a crescendo, the altar seemed to pulse with an otherworldly energy. Shadows, infused with the malevolent forces' influence, danced around the unholy structure, forming a grotesque display of supernatural power. The air became charged with an oppressive force, and the very ground beneath their feet quivered as if in anticipation of the cosmic forces at play.

Ethan, Emma, and Lily, their minds now fully immersed in the visions of the abyss, felt the weight of ancient malevolence pressing down upon them. Samuel, the conduit to the prophecy, saw the threads of destiny converging upon the choices made within the chamber. The family and Samuel, now aware of the gravity of their quest, stood with a collective resolve that defied the encroaching darkness.

"The altar is the conduit through which the malevolent forces draw sustenance," the spectral figure repeated, its form flickering within the shadows. "Confront the darkness within its unholy radiance, and the choices made within this chamber will echo through the corridors of time."

Father Matthias, with unwavering resolve, extended his hands towards the altar. The artifacts in the family's hands emitted a subtle glow that seemed to respond to the ancient structure's awakening. The townsfolk, their faces etched with a mixture of awe and trepidation, watched as the cosmic forces within the chamber reached a fevered pitch.

"The abyss beckons, and the choices made within its unholy radiance will echo through the annals of time," Father Matthias declared, his voice cutting through the supernatural maelstrom. "We stand at the precipice of revelation, and the choices we make within this chamber will determine the fate of this town."

As the altar's unholy radiance intensified, the spectral figure spoke with a sense of both caution and inevitability. "The shadows within the unholy radiance are a reflection of the choices made by those who sought power and salvation. Confront the darkness, and the path to redemption may yet be revealed."

The family and Samuel, their minds now entwined with the artifacts and the unholy radiance of the altar, approached the malevolent structure with a shared determination. The symbols on the altar, infused with the malevolent forces' influence, seemed to respond to the intentions of those who stood before it.

The townsfolk, their eyes fixed on the unfolding drama, held their breath as the family and Samuel stood before the altar. The spectral figure, its form now a mere flicker within the shadows, watched with an intensity that hinted at the mysteries yet to be unveiled.

As the family and Samuel reached out to touch the altar, a surge of energy coursed through the chamber. The shadows around the altar, as if alive, recoiled before reshaping into new configurations. The very air within the chamber seemed to vibrate with the cosmic forces unleashed by the group's touch.

The altar, touched by the hands of those who sought redemption, began to shift and morph. Visions of the abyss and the malevolent entities gave way to a new configuration that spoke of sacrifice and the breaking of ancient curses. The very fabric of the chamber seemed to sigh with the weight of a cosmic transformation.

"The choices made within the heart of the abyss have altered the course of destiny," the spectral figure intoned, its voice carrying a sense of both resignation and hope. "The shadows may yet linger, but the chains that bound this town have been weakened by the courage to confront the darkness within."

The artifacts, now in the hands of the family and Samuel, emitted a final burst of ethereal light before settling into a dormant state. The altar, its unholy radiance subdued, seemed to resonate with the collective will of those who had dared to challenge the malevolent forces.

The chamber, once a battleground of cosmic forces, fell into an eerie stillness. The shadows, though diminished, still clung to the corners, whispering of the malevolent forces that lingered at the edges of perception. The family and Samuel, their faces etched with a mixture of exhaustion and triumph, turned towards Father Matthias with a shared understanding.

"The curse has not been fully broken, but the choices made today have set in motion a new path for this town," Father Matthias declared, his voice carrying a sense of both caution and optimism. "We must press on, confront the remaining shadows within the mansion, and uncover the final key to liberate this town from the grip of darkness."

The townsfolk, now released from the oppressive weight of the curse, looked towards the family and Samuel with a newfound hope. The spectral figure, its form now a mere whisper within the shadows, observed the group with an enigmatic gaze that hinted at the mysteries yet to be unveiled.

The family and Samuel, armed with the artifacts, the knowledge gained from the ancient symbols, the essence of the abyss contained within the dagger, the revelations extracted from the mirror, the incantations deciphered from the tome, the courage to challenge the malevolent forces beyond the gateway, and the triumph over the altar's unholy radiance, prepared to face the final layers of the curse that still lurked within the mansion. The labyrinthine corridors, though still haunted by the echoes of the past, now seemed to hold the promise of redemption.

As the group moved deeper into the mansion, the shadows that clung to the walls seemed to retreat, as if acknowledging the shifting tides of destiny. The artifacts, though dormant, resonated with a subtle energy that guided the way forward. Father Matthias, now a beacon of hope in the midst of the supernatural darkness, led the way with a determination that echoed the collective will of those who sought to break the shackles of damnation.

The haunted mansion, its ancient secrets now partially unveiled, awaited the final confrontation with the shadows that lingered within its forsaken halls. The family and Samuel, united with the townsfolk in a shared quest for redemption, stepped into the unknown with a courage that defied the malevolent forces that sought to resist the dawning light of salvation.

The labyrinthine corridors seemed to whisper with the residue of the supernatural turmoil that had unfolded within the mansion's depths. The family and Samuel, accompanied by a contingent of townsfolk whose newfound hope burned bright, navigated the winding passageways toward the mansion's heart. The artifacts, once aglow with ethereal light, now rested in the hands of Ethan, Emma, Lily, and Samuel, their dormant power held in check for the final confrontation.

Father Matthias, leading the procession, sensed the mounting tension as they approached a grand chamber bathed in an ominous half-light. The air grew thick with the residue of malevolence, and a distant, haunting murmur echoed through the expansive space. As they crossed the threshold, the chamber seemed to pulse with an unholy heartbeat, the walls adorned with grotesque depictions of ancient rituals.

At the center of the room stood an obsidian pedestal, upon which a spectral mist coalesced into an eerie visage—a manifestation of Judas Iscariot himself. The very atmosphere seemed to quiver with the malevolent aura emanating from the figure, and the townsfolk, their newfound hope tinged with trepidation, looked to Father Matthias for guidance.

"The final confrontation awaits us," Father Matthias declared, his voice steady, a pillar of resolve against the encroaching darkness. "Judas Iscariot, the architect of this curse, awaits our challenge. We must be prepared for the abyss to gaze back at us."

The spectral figure of Judas, its form contorted with malevolence, sneered at the intruders. "Fools who dare to challenge the designs of destiny. I am the shadow that stretches across time, and this town is but a pawn in the cosmic game. You cannot escape the fate that awaits."

Ethan, Emma, Lily, and Samuel felt the artifacts in their hands stir with latent power, as if resonating with the looming confrontation. The symbols etched into the artifacts seemed to flicker with the promise of both salvation and damnation. The townsfolk, standing behind Father Matthias, watched with a mixture of awe and fear as the cosmic forces gathered in the chamber.

Father Matthias raised the torch high, its flickering flame casting long, dancing shadows across the chamber. "Judas, your reign of darkness ends here. The choices made by those who seek redemption shall unravel the threads of your malevolence. We stand united against the abyss that you have unleashed upon this town."

Judas' spectral laughter reverberated through the chamber, a dissonant melody that sent shivers down the spines of those present. "Redemption is a fleeting illusion. The abyss is eternal, and your futile resistance merely hastens your descent. Behold the culmination of your choices!"

The obsidian pedestal trembled as the spectral mist surrounding Judas began to weave itself into grotesque forms. The very air within the chamber seemed to distort, creating an otherworldly stage for the impending confrontation. Shadows danced along the edges, their movements synchronized with the malevolent presence of Judas.

Ethan, Emma, Lily, and Samuel, their minds now attuned to the artifacts, saw visions of the abyss converging upon the chamber. The malevolent entities, dark echoes of Judas' betrayal, clawed at the edges of perception, seeking release into the material realm. Samuel, the conduit to the prophecy, felt the weight of ancient power coursing through the chamber, whispering of the final choices that would determine the town's ultimate fate.

Father Matthias, undeterred by the spectral theatrics, raised the artifacts in his hands. "The artifacts hold the power to bind or release the forces that dwell within the abyss. The choices we make now will echo through the corridors of time, shaping the destiny of this town."

The symbols on the artifacts began to glow with an ethereal light, their radiance pushing back against the encroaching shadows. The very fabric of reality seemed to warp as the artifacts became conduits for the ancient power hidden within them. The townsfolk, witnessing the unfolding spectacle, held their collective breath, caught between awe and terror.

Judas, sensing the artifacts' awakening, snarled with renewed malevolence. "You wield the remnants of forgotten power, but the abyss is insatiable. It hungers for the choices that will tip the balance in favor of damnation."

Father Matthias, his voice resonating with both conviction and uncertainty, addressed the family and Samuel. "The artifacts can be used to seal the abyss or unleash its malevolence. Choose wisely, for the fate of this town rests upon the choices we make in this moment."

Ethan, Emma, Lily, and Samuel felt the weight of responsibility pressing down upon them. The artifacts, once dormant tools, now pulsed with a cosmic energy that awaited their command. The symbols on the artifacts seemed to whisper ancient incantations, urging the family and Samuel to make choices that transcended the boundaries of time.

Judas, his spectral form now a writhing maelstrom of darkness, taunted the group. "Make your choices, mortal fools. The abyss cares not for your futile attempts at salvation. Choose, and witness the unraveling of your destiny."

The family and Samuel, their minds entwined with the artifacts, faced the culmination of their journey. The choices they were about to make would either seal the abyss or unleash its malevolent forces upon the town. The grand chamber, caught in a cosmic standstill, waited with bated breath for the decisions that would shape the town's fate.

Ethan, Emma, Lily, and Samuel, their hearts synchronized with the artifacts, looked to each other with a shared understanding. The symbols on the artifacts seemed to guide them, their ethereal glow casting a soft radiance that contrasted with the encroaching shadows.

The townsfolk, witnessing the pivotal moment, held their collective breath. Father Matthias, his eyes locked with the swirling darkness that was Judas, raised the torch higher, its flame now a defiant beacon against the cosmic turmoil.

"Choose, and let the echoes of your choices resonate through the annals of time," Judas intoned, his voice a dissonant harmony that echoed through the chamber.

Ethan, Emma, Lily, and Samuel, their minds unified in purpose, raised the artifacts high. The symbols on the artifacts glowed with an intensity that pushed back against the malevolent forces. The choice was made, and the cosmic forces within the artifacts responded with a surge of ancient power.

The abyss, sensing the artifacts' choice, seemed to convulse with a primal energy. The very fabric of the chamber rippled as the malevolent entities clawed at the boundaries of their supernatural prison. Judas, his spectral form contorting with rage, unleashed a howl that reverberated through the chamber.

"The die is cast," Father Matthias declared, his voice cutting through the cosmic tumult. "The choices made within this moment will determine the town's fate."

As the artifacts emitted a final burst of ethereal light, the abyss, caught in the throes of the artifacts' chosen path, seemed to recede. The malevolent entities, denied release, faded into the shadows, their spectral forms dissipating like smoke in the wind.

Judas, his spectral figure now a mere echo within the chamber, howled with impotent fury. "You may delay the inevitable, but the abyss will persist. Your choices only prolong the town's descent into darkness."

The family and Samuel, their minds still resonating with the artifacts' chosen path, turned towards Father Matthias with a mixture of exhaustion and triumph. The townsfolk, released from the oppressive weight of the curse, looked upon the family and Samuel with a newfound sense of gratitude.

"The abyss has been held at bay, if only for a time," Father Matthias proclaimed, his voice carrying the weight of the ancient power that had coursed through the chamber. "We must now confront the shadows that remain within the mansion and bring an end to the curse that has plagued this town for too long."

The family and Samuel, armed with the artifacts and the knowledge gained from their harrowing journey, moved forward with a shared determination. The labyrinthine corridors, though still haunted by the echoes of the past, now seemed to beckon with the promise of redemption.

As the group ventured further into the mansion, the encroaching darkness seemed to retreat, as if acknowledging the triumph over the abyss. The artifacts, now at rest in the hands of the family and Samuel, resonated with a subtle energy that guided the way forward. Father Matthias, a beacon of hope in the midst of the supernatural darkness, led the way with a determination that echoed the collective will of those who sought to break the shackles of damnation.

The haunted mansion, its ancient secrets now unveiled and its abyssal forces temporarily subdued, awaited the final confrontation with the shadows that lingered within its forsaken halls. The family and Samuel, united with the townsfolk in a shared quest for redemption, stepped into the unknown with a courage that defied the malevolent forces that sought to resist the dawning light of salvation.

And so, the echoes of the abyss lingered in the mansion's depths, a reminder of the choices made and the paths yet to be traversed. The family and Samuel pressed on, resolved to confront the remaining shadows and bring an end to the curse that had ensnared the town for generations. The labyrinthine corridors whispered with the secrets of the past, and the artifacts, now dormant but charged with ancient power, held the key to the town's salvation. The final chapter of their harrowing journey awaited, and the town's fate hung in the delicate balance between light and shadow.

As the family and Samuel ventured deeper into the mansion, the air seemed to thicken with a palpable tension. The artifacts, now dormant in their hands, retained a subtle resonance that pulsed with the lingering power of the chosen path. Father Matthias, his torch casting flickering shadows on the labyrinthine walls, led the way with a steady determination.

The group entered a chamber whose walls were adorned with ancient tapestries, depicting scenes of arcane rituals and foreboding prophecies. The symbols on the artifacts glowed faintly, reacting to the esoteric energies that permeated the room. Father Matthias, his gaze sweeping across the ominous depictions, spoke with a sense of urgency.

"We are approaching the heart of the mansion, where the shadows cling most tenaciously. The remaining curses must be confronted, and the artifacts hold the key to unraveling the malevolence that lingers."

Ethan, Emma, Lily, and Samuel, their minds still resonating with the choices made, felt a renewed sense of purpose. The artifacts, though dormant, seemed to guide them toward the epicenter of the lingering darkness. The townsfolk, now bolstered by the recent triumph over the abyss, followed with a determination that mirrored their leaders'.

The chamber unfolded into a vast hall, its ceiling shrouded in darkness. At the far end, an altar, bathed in a sickly glow, held a spectral presence—a fragment of the abyss that resisted dissolution. Shadows seemed to dance around the altar, and the air hummed with a disquieting energy.

Father Matthias, raising the torch higher, surveyed the scene. "The remnants of the abyss linger here. The shadows are a testament to the malevolence that has gripped this mansion for far too long. We must confront the final vestiges and free this town from the clutches of darkness."

As the group approached the spectral altar, the symbols on the artifacts began to react with an ethereal glow. The family and Samuel, now attuned to the artifacts' ancient power, exchanged determined glances. Father Matthias, positioned at the forefront, took a deep breath before addressing the looming malevolence.

"Shadows that defy the light, your time is at an end. The choices made within the abyss have set in motion a reckoning, and we stand united against the remnants of your curse. The artifacts bear witness to our resolve."

The spectral presence around the altar seemed to quiver, as if aware of the impending confrontation. A whispering darkness echoed through the hall, carrying echoes of ancient incantations and tormented murmurs. The townsfolk, their collective breath held, watched as the family and Samuel raised the artifacts in unison.

Ethan, Emma, Lily, and Samuel, their minds synchronized with the artifacts, felt a surge of energy coursing through them. The symbols on the artifacts, aglow with an otherworldly radiance, seemed to merge with the spectral presence at the altar. The choice made within the abyss now extended its influence to the final remnants of the curse.

The spectral figure, once defiant, now trembled within the shadows. "Your defiance is but a fleeting moment within the tapestry of time. The shadows are eternal, and your feeble attempts at liberation only deepen the despair that awaits."

Father Matthias, undeterred by the malevolent taunts, spoke with unwavering resolve. "The artifacts bear witness to the choices made. We confront the shadows not in fear, but with the courage to shape our destiny. Your time within this realm is ending."

As the artifacts emitted a pulsating energy, the spectral presence at the altar convulsed. The shadows that clung to the hall seemed to writhe in agony, resisting the impending dissolution. The air vibrated with the cosmic forces at play, and the townsfolk, their faces etched with a mixture of awe and trepidation, bore witness to the final confrontation.

"The choices made echo through the corridors of destiny," Samuel intoned, his voice carrying the weight of the prophecy. "The artifacts hold the power to sever the lingering shadows or bind them to the abyss. The town's fate rests upon the choices we make now."

Ethan, Emma, Lily, and Samuel, their hearts intertwined with the artifacts, faced the altar with a shared determination. The symbols on the artifacts seemed to weave a spectral tapestry that connected the family and Samuel to the very fabric of the mansion's ancient curse.

The spectral figure, sensing the artifacts' influence, unleashed a final howl of defiance. "You may shatter the shadows, but the abyss endures. Your choices merely delay the inevitable descent into darkness. Witness the futility of your struggle!"

As the family and Samuel raised the artifacts high, the symbols on the artifacts emitted a blinding radiance. The entire hall seemed to quake as the artifacts' chosen path collided with the lingering malevolence. The spectral figure, engulfed in the ethereal glow, contorted in a spectral tempest.

The townsfolk shielded their eyes from the blinding light, their breaths caught in a collective gasp. Father Matthias, with the torch held high, stood undeterred, his gaze fixed upon the unfolding cosmic spectacle.

The artifacts' energy, now a vortex of ancient power, surged towards the spectral altar. The remnants of the abyss convulsed, caught between dissolution and defiance. Shadows retreated, dissipating into the tapestry of the ancient walls, as if acknowledging the artifacts' chosen path.

Ethan, Emma, Lily, and Samuel, their minds entwined with the artifacts, felt the surge of power extend from their hands into the very essence of the mansion. The spectral figure, its form now a mere wisp within the lingering radiance, emitted a final, haunting whisper.

"The abyss may linger, but your choices have shifted the balance. The shadows fade, but the echoes of your destiny will endure."

As the artifacts' radiance subsided, the hall fell into an eerie stillness. The altar, once bathed in a sickly glow, now stood dormant, devoid of the malevolent presence that had clung to it for generations. The family and Samuel, their faces etched with a mixture of exhaustion and triumph, turned towards Father Matthias.

"The curse has been broken," Father Matthias declared, his voice resonating with the echoes of the artifacts' chosen path. "We have confronted the shadows and severed the final vestiges of the abyss. The town is free."

The townsfolk, released from the oppressive weight of the curse, erupted into cheers. The haunted mansion, its ancient secrets now unveiled and its malevolent forces dispersed, seemed to exhale a collective sigh of relief. The artifacts, though dormant, radiated with a residual energy that hinted at the ancient power they held.

"The choices made within the abyss have shaped our destiny," Samuel said, his gaze fixed upon the artifacts. "But our journey is not yet complete. There is still one task left—the final key to ensure the town's lasting liberation."

Father Matthias nodded, his eyes reflecting a sense of both caution and determination. "The artifacts have revealed the path forward, but the town's salvation requires one last revelation. We must uncover the final key hidden within the mansion's depths and bring an end to this chapter of darkness."

As the family and Samuel, accompanied by the jubilant townsfolk, prepared to embark on the final leg of their harrowing journey, the haunted mansion stood as a testament to the choices made within its forsaken halls. The labyrinthine corridors, though still tinged with echoes of the past, beckoned with the promise of redemption.

The family, armed with the artifacts and guided by the revelations gained from their journey, faced the unknown with a shared determination. The town's fate hung in the delicate balance between the lingering shadows and the burgeoning light of salvation.

And so, the final chapter awaited—a chapter that would unveil the mysteries concealed within the mansion's depths and determine whether the town would remain ensnared by the tendrils of darkness or emerge into the dawn of a new era. The family and Samuel, now united with the townsfolk in a shared quest for lasting liberation, ventured into the heart of the mansion with a courage that defied the echoes of the abyss. The tale, though wrought with darkness, held the promise of redemption—a promise that would be revealed within the uncharted corridors of the mansion's final secrets.

As the family, Samuel, and the jubilant townsfolk ventured further into the mansion, a hushed reverence settled over the labyrinthine corridors. The artifacts, though dormant, seemed to vibrate with anticipation as if attuned to the final revelation awaiting them. Father Matthias, leading the procession with the torch held high, spoke with a measured gravitas.

"We stand on the precipice of the mansion's deepest secrets. The artifacts have guided us this far, and within these walls lies the final key to our town's salvation. Be vigilant, for the shadows may still cling to the hidden recesses."

The group entered a chamber adorned with ancient symbols etched into the walls. The artifacts in the family's hands, responding to the cryptic markings, emitted a subtle glow. Father Matthias surveyed the room with a discerning gaze, his eyes scanning for clues within the arcane patterns.

"The symbols on the walls are a language of the ancients," Father Matthias explained. "They speak of the final key, a culmination of the choices made and the cosmic forces at play. We must decipher their meaning to unveil the path forward."

Ethan, Emma, Lily, and Samuel, their minds still resonating with the artifacts' ancient power, approached the symbols with a shared determination. The townsfolk, now part of a collective quest for redemption, watched with a mix of curiosity and anticipation.

As the family and Samuel examined the symbols, a faint hum resonated through the chamber. The artifacts, seemingly recognizing the language of the ancients, emitted a harmonic resonance that seemed to harmonize with the symbols on the walls. The air became charged with an otherworldly energy, hinting at the unveiling of long-concealed truths.

Father Matthias, his gaze fixed upon the artifacts, spoke with a knowing certainty. "The symbols and the artifacts are intertwined—a cosmic dance of language and power. Together, they will reveal the final key that has eluded us thus far."

The family and Samuel, guided by the artifacts' resonance, began to decipher the symbols' hidden meanings. Visions flashed before their eyes, images of the town's history intertwined with cosmic forces that transcended mortal understanding. The artifacts, now glowing with an ethereal light, seemed to unlock the secrets encoded within the symbols.

"The final key lies within the town's founding, a convergence of celestial energies that shaped its destiny," Samuel intoned, his voice echoing the revelations whispered by the artifacts. "We must trace the threads of the ancients to uncover the truth hidden within the mansion's heart."

Father Matthias nodded, his expression a mixture of reverence and determination. "The town's origin holds the answers we seek. The artifacts will guide us through the corridors of time, revealing the choices made by those who first laid the foundations of our home."

As the family, Samuel, and Father Matthias followed the artifacts' glow, they found themselves in a hidden chamber, its walls adorned with a mural that depicted the town's founding. Celestial bodies, ancient symbols, and a convergence of cosmic forces painted a tapestry of the town's mystical origin.

"The mural tells a tale of cosmic alignment and choices made within the celestial embrace," Father Matthias explained, his fingers tracing the symbols on the walls. "We must understand the significance of the founding moment—the nexus where mortal choices intersected with the forces beyond."

Ethan, Emma, Lily, and Samuel, their minds immersed in the mural's cosmic narrative, felt a connection to the artifacts that transcended the present moment. The symbols on the artifacts, now in perfect harmony with the mural, seemed to resonate with the celestial energies depicted in the ancient painting.

As Father Matthias continued to decipher the mural, a revelation unfolded—a celestial event known as the "Nexus Convergence," a rare alignment of stars and celestial bodies that occurred at the town's founding. The mural hinted at choices made by the town's founders, choices that influenced the cosmic forces at play.

"The Nexus Convergence is a celestial phenomenon that occurs once in a millennium," Father Matthias explained. "The choices made during this alignment shape the destiny of the town and determine its connection to the cosmic forces beyond."

Samuel, now attuned to the artifacts and the mural's revelations, spoke with a sense of conviction. "The town's destiny is entwined with the Nexus Convergence. The artifacts, guided by the choices we've made, hold the key to unlocking the cosmic forces that shape our fate."

The family and Samuel, their resolve deepened by the newfound understanding, raised the artifacts high. The symbols on the artifacts seemed to interact with the celestial energies depicted in the mural. A surge of ancient power flowed through the chamber, as if bridging the gap between the mortal realm and the cosmic forces that lay beyond.

Father Matthias, witnessing the artifacts' resonance with the mural, spoke with a reverence that transcended the earthly plane. "The artifacts have become conduits for the cosmic forces. The choices made within the Nexus Convergence will either bind the town to the shadows or liberate it into the light."

The artifacts emitted a radiant glow, harmonizing with the celestial energies depicted in the mural. The air itself seemed to shimmer with the convergence of mortal choices and cosmic destinies. The townsfolk, now assembled in the hidden chamber, held their breath in awe of the unfolding cosmic spectacle.

Ethan, Emma, Lily, and Samuel, their minds entwined with the artifacts and the celestial energies, felt a weight of responsibility. The symbols on the artifacts, now aglow with an ethereal brilliance, seemed to channel the power of the Nexus Convergence. The family and Samuel, their hearts synchronized with the cosmic forces, faced the mural with a shared determination.

"The choices made within the Nexus Convergence will determine the town's destiny," Samuel declared, his voice echoing through the hidden chamber. "We must guide the artifacts to align with the forces of light, severing the shackles that bind the town to the shadows."

As the artifacts emitted a pulsating energy, the mural's celestial figures seemed to come to life. The Nexus Convergence, once a distant memory, manifested within the chamber, as if the cosmic forces themselves were present to witness the choices about to be made.

Father Matthias, his eyes fixed upon the artifacts and the mural, raised the torch high. "The Nexus Convergence responds to the artifacts' chosen path. The town's fate is in our hands, and we must ensure that the choices made within this moment bring an end to the shadows that linger."

The family and Samuel, now enveloped in the radiant glow of the artifacts, directed the celestial energies towards the mural. The symbols on the artifacts danced in harmony with the cosmic forces, weaving a tapestry of light that pushed back against the lingering shadows.

"The Nexus Convergence acknowledges the choices made by those who hold the artifacts," Father Matthias intoned, his voice carrying the weight of ancient prophecies. "Guide the celestial energies to align with the forces of redemption, and witness the liberation of the town from the clutches of darkness."

Ethan, Emma, Lily, and Samuel, their minds focused on the artifacts' chosen path, felt the surge of ancient power reach its crescendo. The Nexus Convergence, now an ethereal symphony, responded to the artifacts' alignment with a burst of cosmic brilliance.

The mural, once static, seemed to ripple with the celestial energies. The shadows that clung to the hidden chamber retreated, as if banished by the harmonizing forces of light. The artifacts, now aglow with a transcendent radiance, held the town's destiny within their ethereal embrace.

As the cosmic energies subsided, the hidden chamber fell into an enchanted stillness. The mural, now an illuminated testament to the choices made within the Nexus Convergence, radiated with a cosmic brilliance that transcended mortal understanding.

"The Nexus Convergence has responded to the artifacts' chosen path," Father Matthias proclaimed, his voice resonating with a sense of both awe and reverence. "The town's destiny has been shaped by the choices made within this cosmic alignment. We have unveiled the final key to redemption."

The townsfolk, witnessing the cosmic spectacle, erupted into cheers. The haunted mansion, its ancient secrets now unveiled and its cosmic forces aligned with the artifacts, seemed to exhale a collective sigh of relief. The family and Samuel, their faces etched with a mixture of exhaustion and triumph, turned towards Father Matthias.

"The town is free from the shadows that lingered within the Nexus Convergence," Father Matthias declared, his voice carrying the echoes of the artifacts' chosen path. "We have completed the journey and confronted the ancient curses that ensnared our home. The final key has been unveiled, and the town is now poised for a new era of redemption."

The family and Samuel, their minds still resonating with the artifacts' ancient power, faced the jubilant townsfolk with a shared sense of accomplishment. The labyrinthine corridors, though still tinged with echoes of the past, now seemed to beckon with the promise of a town reborn.

As the group prepared to exit the hidden chamber and emerge from the mansion's depths, the artifacts, though now dormant, retained a subtle glow. The symbols on the artifacts seemed to whisper of the ancient power that had coursed through them, and the family and Samuel, now united with the townsfolk in a shared quest for lasting liberation, stepped into the unknown with a courage that defied the echoes of the abyss.

The haunted mansion, its ancient curses lifted and its final key unveiled, stood as a testament to the choices made and the cosmic forces that had shaped its destiny. The family and Samuel, now guided by the artifacts' transcendent glow, moved forward into the awaiting dawn of a new era for the town.

And so, the echoes of the abyss faded into the shadows, replaced by the resonating harmony of redemption. The labyrinthine corridors whispered with the secrets of the past, and the artifacts, though dormant, held the key to the town's enduring liberation. The tale, wrought with darkness and cosmic forces, unfolded with the promise of a town reborn into the light.